MW00642189

This Property Is Condemned

Book #4 in The Sam Cooper Adventure Series

This Property Is Condemned

Book #4 in The Sam Cooper Adventure Series

Max Elliott Anderson

Elk Lake
Publishing, Inc.

Elk Lake Publishing

This Property is Condemned
Sam Cooper Adventure Series #4
Copyright © 2016 by Max Elliott Anderson

Requests for information should be addressed to:
Elk Lake Publishing, 35 Dogwood Dr, Plymouth, MA 02360
ISBN-13 Number: 978-1-944430-30-6

Graphics Design: Anna M. O'Brien
Editors: Kathi Macias, Deb Haggerty
Published in Association with Hartline Literary Agency

Dedicated to Grace Kathryne and Olivia McKenzie

Chapter 1

No Brakes

"Look out below! I got no brakes!" Sam Cooper shrieked as he plummeted down the one and only steep hill in Harper's Inlet riding the rustiest, most beat up old bike anyone had seen in a long time. But there was no place to hide, no place to turn around and certainly no way he could possibly stop this deathtrap short of crashing into something. That thought sent a chill up Sam's back, which was kind of funny because sweat already flowed like a fountain from his forehead. He grasped the handlebars with the force of two vise-grips. Every bone in his hands stuck out, threatening to burst right through his suntanned skin. For the first time in his short life, Sam understood what white knuckles really meant. If he cared to look down, which he didn't, he was sure to see two sets of them poking back up at him.

"Aim for the grass!" Tony Dodds yelled from about three bike lengths behind. Next to Tony, a terrified Tyler Peterson raced headlong down the same hill. But then, his bike *had* brakes.

With a quick glance, Sam called back over his shoulder, "I thought you said you fixed this dumb thing," His chest tightened and his breathing became rapid. All he could think about was how this wouldn't be happening to him if he had a decent bike, only he didn't have a lot of time to think about that right now.

"I did fix it," Tony assured him. "Now aim for the grass like I told ya and you won't get hurt."

"Easy for you to say," Sam grumbled. "You guys have brakes!" Now he began to sweat all over. His hands became so cold and wet they nearly slipped right off of the rubber handgrips.

"My fingers are going numb," Sam cried out. If he had time to think about it, he would have remembered how much he had hated that old bike in the first place. Right now he was pretty angry with his father. *Really, would a new bike cost that much? I mean, it's not like I'm asking for a car or anything. And it has to be cheaper than the hospital bill I'm gonna get.* As his eyes flashed up ahead, stopping wasn't exactly his first priority. It looked like several other terrible things were about to happen before that. It seemed impossible, but Sam felt like his bike was picking up speed. *Piece of junk!*

"It's the best I can do for now," his father had told him when he'd first brought the bike home. "We'll go shopping for a new one after we get settled here." But his new job had taken way more time than he'd expected and then he'd had his heart attack.

THIS PROPERTY IS CONDEMNED

How come this is the best one he could find? One of the pedals was bent, the fenders had big dents, he needed a new seat and, worst of all, the thing didn't have any *brakes!*

Sam's eyes darted to both sides as he approached Bay Street. Fortunately, he had traveled up and down this hill a couple of times before. That's why he knew there was no escape until they reached the bottom. But he also knew there could be a lot of traffic on the way down. If he and a car came to the same intersection at the same time, his bike was going to lose that battle.

Whew, no cars coming. He let out a deep sigh, which allowed him to catch his breath for an instant and relax his grip on the handlebars just a little. That was nanoseconds before he saw Mr. Elkins backing out of his driveway in the middle of the next block. A sick feeling came to his stomach. That feeling reminded him of something else he tried not to think about too much. Sam had a secret. Even his best friends didn't know what it was. If people knew, maybe they wouldn't help him like they did where he used to live. He hoped no one ever found out about it.

Mr. Elkins never stopped his minivan to look both ways. As usual, he just kept backing out of the driveway like this was a normal day on a normal street with nothing to worry about.

Sam screamed out in terror, "Now what?"

"Start hollering," Tyler said.

"I could have thought of that one *all* by myself," Sam called back. Then he yelled so loud that people came out of their houses to see what was wrong. Except for the traffic, this was usually a pretty quiet street. Not today, not at this moment, and right now Sam was in serious trouble. All three boys called out their warnings.

"Stop!" Tyler warned. But his voice only came out in squeaks that sounded a lot like the awful noises a violin makes when someone first starts taking lessons.

And Tony added, "Get out-a-the-way!" Just the sound of his voice almost made Sam mad because it was Tony who had told him the brakes should work now after he tightened them. How was Sam going to miss the old man's minivan without any bike brakes?

But now it was too late. That's because Mr. Elkins couldn't hear very well. It didn't matter how loud the boys yelled. Even on a good day, he wouldn't know if a shotgun had gone off in the back seat unless his hearing aid was turned up to high and it had new batteries. Sam wondered how the old man kept passing his driving test.

Funny I'd think of a thing like that at a time like this. Sam wasn't sure how, but he barely managed to avoid the front bumper of the Elkins van, darted between two garbage cans, missed hitting a cat by less than a whisker, and found himself back on the sidewalk. He let out the deep breath he'd been holding in for nearly a block. That's all the time he had before the next hazard. By now he flew so fast, he figured any paint that was still left on that old rusted wreck-of-a-bike would start flying off for sure.

Not far ahead, Sam spotted a mailman who probably thought he was delivering mail on a typical day where the worst thing he had to face was a vicious dog or two. He carried a can of spray to keep them away, but nothing could have prepared him for what was about to happen. The poor man made the mistake of stepping out of his truck only seconds before this trio of torpedoes reached him. Three streaks flew past in less than an eye blink. As he jumped back, his arms flew up sending a full pouch of letters, brochures, and magazines flying in all directions.

Tony looked back and called out, "Air mail!" His friends laughed, but the mailman didn't. He waved his arms in the air as he let them know what kind of madmen he thought they were. But the boys were already too far away to apologize.

With less than a minute left until certain disaster, Sam was faced with a decision. A lot like the choice a quarterback has to make when he wants to pass, but there are three gigantic players charging toward him and no one is open. Sam had only a few split-second choices too. Should he aim for the rose bushes, a brick wall, or the rusty, old fence dead ahead?

Rose bushes have thorns. Bad idea. He already knew this because his mother grew beautiful roses in the backyard of every house where they had lived. He remembered the first time, when he was very young, he discovered what thorns were. *And I know what happens to anything that hits a brick wall. The wall always wins.* He chose to aim his bike toward the double-high chain-link fence directly in front of him. Now he could only hope and pray that there wouldn't be any cars crossing when Landon Hill Road came to a T with Shore Drive at the bottom of the hill.

His bike shot through the intersection. *Whew, no traffic.*

"Use your feet," Tyler warned, but it was too late for that. His front wheel hit the curb and launched Sam and his bike high into the air. He simply put his head down, closed his eyes and thought about his short life. Suddenly Sam hit the fence like an NFL fullback. From behind he could hear his friends skidding to a stop in loose gravel. *No fair, they've got brakes that work.* He had fully expected to splatter up against the fence like a bug on the windshield of his dad's car, but something else happened instead. It almost seemed like his world went into slow motion for a time. He felt his body grind to a temporary stop before it shot back off. The chain link fence reminded him of a trampoline he used to play on at a neighbor's house before they had it taken out. Or the practice net a kicker uses on a football team just before he's called on to kick the winning field goal. In his mind, Sam saw himself in the shape of a tennis ball with a face, arms, legs, and wearing *his* clothes as it crashed into a racket and bounced back off.

Huh? No sooner had that thought rocketed through his brain than he felt himself flying back the other way. Sam opened one eye just to make sure he was still alive and hoped it was only a dream. This was a mistake because, at that very instant, he glanced *down* at Tony and Tyler while he flew over their heads.

Yikes, this is just like the dream I keep having where I really can fly.

As he looked … they ducked and Sam barely skimmed over the tops of their heads. When he opened his other eye, he saw a post coming right at him. The post had a sign but the writing was on the other side. Sam tucked in his right leg and shoulder, missing the post by less than an inch. Then he finally hit the ground and rolled to a stop.

THIS PROPERTY IS CONDEMNED

Tyler was the first to whimper. "Is he dead?"

But Tony couldn't help laughing. "That's the funniest thing I've ever seen. If God wanted us to fly …" But he didn't finish that sentence. It might have been because of the look of anger on his friend's face.

Sam got to his feet and began moving toward Tony. Only his legs were still a little wobbly underneath his sweating body.

"I'm dead," Tony said. He began stepping backward until he fell over a small shrub but Sam's look went right past him.

"What's wrong with you?" Tyler asked.

"I hate that stupid bike," Sam fumed. "Just once I wish my dad would …" Before he finished, he reached his poor excuse for a bike, drew his leg back and kicked the front fender as hard as he could. A sharp pain radiated from his big toe all the way to the top of his head and back down to his toe again. He began jumping up and down on his good foot while howling at the top of his voice until he'd hopped back past the sign again.

"You keep dancing around like that … it's gonna rain for sure," Tony said.

Finally, Sam fell in a heap near the post and rubbed his throbbing foot. The last time he had ever felt such pain was back when he and his friends barely made it through the storm that spit them out again on Lost Island. But he couldn't concentrate on that right now.

"Next time the garbage truck comes by my house, that bike's gettin' a first class ticket."

Tyler shook his head. "But then you wouldn't have a bike at all."

Sam gave him an angry stare. "I don't have one now." He turned and pointed back at the wheel that still spun around. "That piece of junk's a death trap." He took a deep breath. "It needs to be buried in the landfill ... forever!

"We should get Mr. Kincaid to fix it up for you," Tony said. "He can fix anything."

"Well, I'm never letting *you* touch it again, that's for sure. I don't know how, but one of these days I'm gettin' a new bike." Then he looked up at the sign on the post that nearly took his life. "Hey you guys, look at this." Sam pointed to the lettering.

His friends dropped their bikes and rushed to where he stood.

Tyler read slowly. "This property is ... condemned."

"What's that mean?" Tony asked.

"I heard that word on the news a couple weeks ago, so I asked my dad about it," Sam said. "He told me about some of the criminals that hafta be locked up."

"Boy," Tony said, "that must be so cool to put people in jail. Cops are lucky."

Sam shook his head as he rubbed the back of his neck. "That's not the way he said it. He told me about how guys have been condemned to die for crimes they've done."

Tyler's eyes blinked and he shuddered. "You think somebody like that's around here?"

Sam shook his head again. "The sign doesn't mean it that way."

Tony scratched his head. "What then?"

"I don't know, but I'm gonna find out."

Chapter 2

Mysterious Mansion

No one realized it at first, but they were standing outside of the old Remmington estate. Sam hadn't really seen it before so the first thing he noticed about the place was the rusty fence that protected the property for as far as he could see in both directions. He and his friends had ridden their bikes past the old place a few times and no one paid much attention to it until now. Looking through the fence, Sam could barely even make out the shape of a house because of all the brush and dense trees that covered everything. Sam knew he'd be in trouble if he ever let his yard get so overgrown. One of his main jobs was to keep the grass cut and to trim the bushes at his house.

Tony shielded his eyes from the bright, hot sun, pressed his face into the fence and asked, "Think anybody still lives in there?"

Sam leaned down and rubbed his sore toe again. "How should I know? You're the guys who live here." He wiped some of the sweat off of his face with the top of his shirt and stared back toward the house. "I don't know why anybody'd want to stay in a place as creepy as that."

Tony turned toward him and squinted. Then, with a slight smile he said, "Well, you're the one who's always tryin' to figure things out."

Sam continued looking toward the rundown mansion nearly hidden among the trees. "Maybe I will."

Sam's two friends knew most of what went on in their small, coastal town. They'd already told him some of the stories when they came over to his house. But no one had said anything about that old place before.

Tyler kept his eyes fixed toward the mansion. "Is it true that somebody really got killed in the basement?" As he held onto the fence, he shuddered, his eyes blinked, and his hands shook the entire section in front of them. It caused some of the loose metal to rub against the poles, creating an eerie sound that made the house seem even creepier.

Tony turned to Tyler. "Yeah, and what about the old lady that used to live in there? Didn't she die or something?"

Tyler shook his head. Tony went on to say there had been a lot of stories about the Remmington Mansion. But those stories seemed to get bigger, the more people told them.

Right now Sam had other things to think about. He limped over, reached down, pulled up what was left of his bike and dragged it toward the sidewalk. "The front rim's bent. I'll have to push it home."

16

"Good thing," Tony snickered. "It's too dangerous to ride anyway."

Sam gave him one of those looks again. It was the kind that said, "Don't tempt me." His friends picked their bikes up off the ground and walked them alongside Sam's. They started up the hill without talking. All Sam could think about was how he had just escaped one of the most dangerous events of his life. His father had always told him things happen for a reason in life. That thought sent several others racing through his head. Then he stopped, turned around and looked back toward the mansion one last time.

"Forget something back there?" Tyler asked as he looked back too.

"Yeah," Tony said with a laugh, "he forgot to stop."

Sam ignored that comment and continued staring back.

"Let's take your bike over to Kincaid's place," Tyler said. "He'll know how to fix it."

Sam snapped his head around. "Fix it? There's no way in the world anyone could do that."

"Kincaid can," Tyler said. "He can fix anything."

"Who's this Kincaid guy?"

Tony smiled back. "You'll see."

The three friends pushed their bikes up Landon Hill Road and toward a small junkyard near the edge of town. It was one of those places with a high fence, but everything in it and around it was either rusty, dusty, or dented. The tall, board fence might have been painted white at some time in history; only from the way it looked today, that had to be a long time ago. Wind, rain, and the salty sea air made its boards just as beat up as the rest of the junk they protected.

There were spaces between the tall boards where Sam could see old cars, trucks, barrels, and other things made of metal.

Tony told Sam the junkyard had a guard dog named Blitz. And Mr. Kincaid told them that without the dog, people might break in and steal valuable parts. Blitz fit the description of a junkyard dog. He looked like the kind of hound that could tear a man apart just for fun. The sound of his vicious, booming bark kept most sensible people away. But Blitz knew Tony and Tyler, and Tony and Tyler knew Blitz. As they entered the gate, that big dog may as well have been a harmless, toothless puppy. Still, he whined, jumped up on Sam and gave him a sniff and a big slurpy, right in the face.

"Blitz!" Tony scolded as Sam wiped his face and spit on the ground. "Cut it out."

The dog dropped down and followed them as they walked toward a shabby wooden building. Its siding looked just as worn out as the fence.

When Mr. Kincaid saw the boys coming, he finished working at a grinding wheel, where sparks shot into the air, then stopped what he was doing and met them inside the door. He looked down at what was left of Sam's bike. "My, oh my, what happened to her?"

Sam looked down at it, too. "Can you fix this thing?"

"He can fix anything," Tony said with a smile.

Mr. Kincaid continued looking at Sam's battered bike. Then he looked up at Sam. "Don't believe I know you, son."

THIS PROPERTY IS CONDEMNED

Sam held out his hand. "I'm Sam." But when he saw Mr. Kincaid's greasy hand, he slowly dropped his. The old man looked down, pulled a rag from his back pocket and wiped it clean. He looked up to Sam with a smile, "Sorry. I forget sometimes." Sam smiled back.

The old man took off a dirty red hat and wiped beads of sweat from his forehead with the same rag. When he put his oil-stained hat back on, he laughed a little. "I fix things, that's true, but I don't do miracles." He continued studying Sam's pitiful bike. "Now *that* would take a miracle." Then he chuckled again. As he kept looking at what was left of Sam's bike, he walked in a circle all the way around as it lay on the ground where Sam had dropped it in the dirt.

Sam's face turned red. There was that "thing" he'd never told anyone about. He could feel it inside again and he was embarrassed. But that wasn't all. He felt anger inside too. Right now, he was mad at his father for not buying him a decent bike or at least bringing home something better than this one. *No wonder the kid who used to own it dumped the thing in the bushes where my dad found it. Shoulda left it there.* He wondered what his friends must be thinking of him right now. Besides, they both had expensive looking bikes with great paint jobs and gleaming chrome.

Mr. Kincaid picked up the rusty wreck and pushed it into his shop. As he did, the front wheel rolled like a clown's bike at the circus. Each time the flat spot on the rim came around, the front of the bike dipped down ... thump! Then it bounced up again on the good part of the wheel. That didn't help the crummy way Sam already felt.

19

When they reached the workbench, Sam asked, "Do you know anything about the old Remmington place?"

"What's to know?" the old man said.

Sam walked around to the other side of the bike. "You know … the stories and stuff."

Mr. Kincaid took off his hat again and scratched his head through thin, white hair. "Stories are just stories, that's all."

"Is it true that old lady died in there?" Tyler asked. His eyes widened and started blinking again.

Tony tried to act like he wasn't afraid. "I heard the place is haunted. There's guys who went in there and never came out again." He nodded and crossed his arms. "That's what I heard."

"Nonsense." Mr. Kincaid shook his head and took another rag out of the back pocket of his dirty, faded blue overalls with a hole in one knee. Then he sniffed. "She's still in there."

Tony stepped back. "She *is*?" He should have watched where he was going because he crashed into a pile of rusted, empty cans, sending them clattering across the cement floor. It sounded like the entire drumline in the school band had dropped their drums on the sidewalk. He grabbed the edge of a table just in time or he would have gone sprawling right along with those cans into a pool of oil and dirt on the floor.

Tyler and Sam laughed and that helped Sam not to feel so nervous. "You'd make a great bowling ball," Tyler said.

Tony barely blinked as he struggled to get back on his feet. So much for trying to act brave. "You mean somebody actually *lives* in that old house?"

20

THIS PROPERTY IS CONDEMNED

Mr. Kincaid went to work on the front end of Sam's bike. "Indeed they do." He took a wrench and loosened one of the bolts that held the wheel in place. "Why don't you boys come back tomorrow morning? I should have her good as new by then. You can't do much good standing around here watching me work" Then he looked over to where all the cans had scattered. "And I don't need any more help redecorating the place either."

Sam looked at him and grumbled. "I should just push that poor excuse for a bike to the dump."

Mr. Kincaid lowered his wrench and looked up toward the ceiling. "Now, when I was a boy ..."

Tony rolled his eyes and groaned. "Please. Do we have to hear one of your stories from back before you had electricity?"

Mr. Kincaid cleared his throat. "When I was a boy, we saved everything. My mother reused jars and bottles; she kept wire, rubber bands, twine ... everything."

Tony looked around the cluttered shop. "Sorta like this place. Is this all her stuff?"

The old man smiled and shook his head. He put down his wrench on the edge of the workbench. "That's the problem today. People throw everything away and just go out and buy new junk. Most of it's not even made here anymore."

Sam smiled and sighed at the same time. "Just once, I wish that could happen to me. All I get is new old junk." He gave his bike another disgusted look.

"You take this bike here." Mr. Kincaid said.

"No, you take it," Sam joked.

"They don't make 'em like this anymore."

Tyler laughed. "That's for sure."

"Well, sir. The frame is heavier than on your bikes over there. The sprockets are as sound as the day she was built. With a little paint and chrome, this could be a beauty again."

Sam shook his head. "Somehow I can't quite see that."

"Hey, Sam," Tony joked, "I think I hear the dump calling."

"That's because it's calling your name," Tyler told him.

"Like I said," Mr. Kincaid continued, "you boys come back tomorrow. I'll have her ready for you then."

They started to leave when Sam turned back. "And don't forget to fix the brakes; front *and* back. That's how the rim got all bent up in the first place." As he left the shop, he added in a half whisper, "I hate that old thing."

"Old man Kincaid?" Tony asked.

"Of course not."

They began walking back toward Tyler's house. Sam would rather have been riding than walking. He turned to his friends as they pushed their bikes. "What do you guys think about what he said?"

Tony looked over. "Who? About what?"

Sam stopped walking and thought for a moment. "The old lady still living in that house."

"I don't know," Tyler said. "You think she's condemned or something?"

"I told you guys somebody got killed in the basement," Tony reminded them. His voice went up a little higher. "Probably she did it."

That sent a shiver up Sam's back. Right then, he pictured the worst scary movie he'd ever seen with all the bad things that only happen after dark down in basements. In his mind, he even imagined the spooky music that goes along with movies like that. He turned to Tony. "Sometimes you say the strangest things."

"You guys wanna go swimming at my house?" Tyler asked. The sun had been up high for a few hours, the temperature was even higher and sweat poured off everyone. Tyler's pool seemed like a resort on hot, humid days like this.

"Sure," they both answered at the same time.

"Come on over after lunch."

The boys scattered toward their houses. Summer vacation had already given them lots of adventure. But the weather had picked this week to turn up the summer heat so an invitation to the pool came at exactly the right time.

Even though his father didn't live there, Tyler's family owned one of the nicest houses in town. Tony's house was even bigger, but Tyler never made Sam feel bad about not having as much as he and Tony did. They were best friends and best friends don't do that. But Sam still felt it. Even though his father was an important scientist, he knew his family didn't have a lot of money and it bothered him sometimes. Still, Sam's friends knew that if he wanted to, he could raise any amount of money he needed. He'd told them about a couple of towns where he lived before and helped raise money for projects. It's just that he never spent any of it on himself.

When the boys met at the pool later that afternoon, Tyler asked, "So what do you think we should do?"

"Do?" Sam asked as he put his towel on a chair by the edge of the pool.

Tony grinned. "Go swimming, what else?"

"I mean about Mrs. Remmington and her messed-up house."

Both boys turned to Sam as if they knew exactly what he was going to say next. He sat on the edge of the pool and tapped his finger against his chin. Then he stood up and announced, "We should help her fix that old place up. If we did that, nobody could tell her she has to move so they can flatten it."

"But how?" Tony asked. "It sounds like too much work."

"I have an idea," Sam said with a smile. Then, he dove into the water and the others followed.

Chapter 3

Time to Investigate

From what he had told them before, Tony and Tyler both knew if Sam ever got one of his ideas, it was going to mean nothing but work for them. People in Harper's Inlet were beginning to learn that Sam Cooper could get things done. He had a reputation as a confident, self-assured person who wasn't afraid of anything or anyone.

He'd also told his friends that when he was six, it bothered him the way trash littered the main street running right through the middle of his old town. That was because Main Street was also part of a state highway with heavy traffic. Though it was true that some of trash probably came from the cars of drivers who didn't even live in that town, he didn't like others to think that the people didn't care enough about their town to keep it clean.

He told Tony and Tyler he brought all of his friends together. They went to businesses, organizations, churches, and homes to find enough people who could help clean up the trash. Working together, the cleanup army filled six dump trucks with bags and bags of trash. The metals and plastics were separated for recycling. Everything else was trucked to the landfill. Now, each spring, that town still sets aside the first Saturday in May for cleanup. There are always enough people who volunteer. Trucks, trash bags, and time are all donated. The mayor even dedicated it as Sam Cooper Day. After the cleanup, there's a big picnic in the center of town. A television station even came out one year to report on the work.

Then, when he heard the high school needed new football uniforms, Sam sprang into action at the age of eight. He couldn't bear the thought of guys from his town being laughed at when they went to play other schools.

By the time he had finished, not only did the school have all the money they needed for the football uniforms, there was enough left over for basketball and baseball uniforms, and cheerleaders uniforms too. "Me and my friends are gonna play sports when we get to high school," Sam had said at the time. "Then we'll need them too." But he really wasn't a selfish person. He always thought of others first. And he'd moved away from there before high school anyway.

When people saw him coming down the street back then, they automatically reached for their wallets, purses, or checkbooks. Storeowners wondered what materials they'd need to donate for the next project.

THIS PROPERTY IS CONDEMNED

Sam hadn't figured out how to take debit or credit cards yet, but it was only a matter of time before he'd set that up on his smartphone. "I'm working on it," he'd told one of the merchants. Still, he never kept any money for himself, not even for a new bike. Sam wasn't pushy about his fundraising. Something about him just made a person want to give or get involved. People even called him at home, just to see how they could help, when they knew he had a new project.

"You should have your own private line," his mother had teased him a few times.

No matter what grade he was in at school, his class always won the prize for raising the most money, doing the most work, or going far beyond whatever goal had been set. The students were glad he was in their class because of all the prizes they had won over the years. Sam provided the winning edge every time.

"People always aim too low," he'd often say. "Who wants to get involved in something unless you plan to do your best?"

You might say he tried too hard to make a difference. But everyone liked him so much, they didn't mind pitching in.

Any time there was a need, the people knew they could count on Sam Cooper to take care of it. His father liked to tell him, "Right place, right time, right kid." Even the leaders from a few of the surrounding towns and newspaper reporters had come to learn how they might do some of the same projects in their towns. But if it were ever a contest, Sam and Marshfield—the last town where he'd lived—would always win. The citizens of Marshfield were sorry to see Sam and his family move away and now Harper's Inlet was about to find out what this powerhouse could do.

"You got a strange look in your eye," Tyler told Sam as they climbed out of the pool.

"Yeah," Tony complained. "When that happens, I start thinking about what comes next. Work—a whole lotta work."

Sam smiled. "I'll see you guys tomorrow." He picked up his towel, slipped on his sandals and jogged toward home. *Sure wish I had a bike right now.*

The temperature felt so hot against his skin, he wouldn't have minded even if it were his old bike right now. When he sprinted into the garage, he found his father working there. Sam came to a stop but still breathed heavily. He looked down at the garage floor where what used to be a lawnmower now lay scattered in a zillion pieces. A pool of thick, dirty oil had oozed out into a large circle. His father's face, arms, and hands were covered with black grease, which was also smeared all over his clothes.

"Hey, Dad, whatcha doin'?"

His father looked up, wiped grease and sweat from the end of his nose with the back of his hand, which also had grease covering it, took a cloth out of his pocket and wiped his hands. "Well, just trying to get another summer out of this old lawnmower of ours." He looked past his son. "Where's your new bike?"

"New?" Sam asked. He was careful not to let his dad know how he really felt. "Oh," he said as he looked away, "the brakes went out on it."

"What happened?"

"We were on Landon Hill Road."

His father straightened up and raised his eyebrows. "With *no* brakes?"

Sam nodded and let out a deep breath. "I crashed into a fence at the bottom of the hill."

His father stepped closer. "You could have been hurt. Where's the bike now?"

"Some guy named Kincaid has it. Says he can make it good as new. He's a friend of Tony and Tyler's."

His father shook his head and looked down. "I'm sorry, son. Guess I should have been more careful about that before I gave it to you."

"Tony told me he'd fixed the brakes but they still didn't work. It was okay, though, except for the mailman."

"Mailman?"

Sam chuckled. "Never mind, he doesn't deliver in our neighborhood anyway. I really came to ask you a question."

Even though his father was a person who didn't like to spend money unless he absolutely had to, Sam knew the man spent as much time with him as he could.

"Fire away." His father wiped more grease from his arms and waited while Sam walked over and sat on a milk crate.

"Remember when you told me about the word condemned?"

"Sure I do, why?"

Sam pulled his feet back so his tennis shoes wouldn't get into the oil on the floor. "I know what it means for a prisoner, but what does it mean when something says this property is condemned?"

His father smiled and relaxed a little. "Now that's an easy one. Usually it means that a building is in such bad shape, it isn't safe anymore. If no one makes the needed repairs, the building has to come down."

My bike should be condemned. "What happens then?"

"A work crew with heavy equipment and trucks comes in and tears the thing down so something new can be built in its place. A building that's condemned isn't safe for people to live or work in anymore."

"Well," Sam began, "how does a house get condemned? Could it happen to ours?"

His father walked over and sat next to him on another crate. "Not ours. A house is probably condemned because the owner moved away and let the place fall apart or they could be living there and still not take good care of the property."

Sam listened carefully since he knew it was possible someone still lived in the Remmington place.

"At first," his father continued, "the roof might start to leak. If water gets in, it ruins the floors, walls, and ceilings. After that, the place starts falling apart."

Sam leaned forward. "And that means somebody else can come along and just knock the thing down?"

"It isn't quite that simple. First the city tries to get the owner to fix it up. They send out warning letters to encourage them to make repairs to the property. If they make the repairs, then the house or building can stay right where it is." He tilted his head to one side, and looked at Sam. "Hey, why are you asking all these questions?"

"Because, I saw a sign after I finally hit the fence at the bottom of Landon Hill Road …"

"You really hit a fence?" his father asked in alarm.

Sam sighed and nodded. "I didn't want you to worry about it."

"But you're all right … right?"

"Sure, Dad."

"And your bike?"

Sam's voice brightened a little. "Bent the front rim. Mr. Kincaid said I can come back and pick it up tomorrow."

"Well, I'm glad you're okay."

Sam smiled. "Me, too. Which is more than I can say for the lawnmower." They both looked out at all the pieces spread across the floor and laughed. When they stood up, Sam headed for the door and his father went back to work. The lawnmower was just one more example of the junk Sam wished his family didn't have to put up with.

Early the next morning, Sam called Tony and Tyler. They agreed to meet at the park that had swings and other equipment. The boys each sat in a swing and talked.

"What's so important?" Tony grumbled. "I only got to eat half my breakfast. My mom was really mad."

"How do you know that?" Tyler asked.

"Because she was still yelling when I ran out the door."

"I think we should go back to that old house and see if there really is someone living in it." Sam said.

"You nuts?" Tony asked. "I saw as much as I need to of that dump from the street."

Sam looked at him. "Mr. Kincaid says an old lady lives there. What could be so scary about that? And what if she was your grandmother or something?"

"Are you forgetting the basement?" Tony put up his hands and started wiggling all his fingers. He changed his voice to sound like someone in a spooky movie. "Scary things always happen in basements."

"Our house has a basement," Tyler said, "and nothing bad's ever happened down there except once when my mom slammed her hand in the dryer door."

Tony smiled. "Maybe nothing bad since *you've* been alive."

Tyler shook his head. "But my parents built that house."

"The Remmington basement is just a story," Sam said. "And besides, nobody would stay in a house if that really happened."

"Unless she had something to do with it," Tyler said. He let out a nervous laugh. "Right?"

Sam stood up to leave. "Fine. You guys can do whatever you want but I'm going out there." As he started walking away, his friends quickly ran to push their bikes beside him.

Tyler turned to Sam. "At least, let's go get your bike first,"

They hurried over to Mr. Kincaid's shop but when they reached it, the door was locked. Blitz wasn't in the yard either.

"Great," Tony said. "Now what?"

Sam looked around the junkyard. Finally, he saw it over by a storage shed. But it didn't look good as new like the old man had promised. His bike looked just as rusty and old as it ever had.

When they walked through the gate, Sam pointed. "There it is." His heart sank. For some reason, he had imagined that Mr. Kincaid would have done something special—not simply put the same junky bike back together again. Sam climbed onto the old wreck and the boys rode away. His bike still rattled every time it hit a bump just like it did before the crash. Soon they came to a stop at the top of Landon Hill Road.

Tony looked down the street. "Think you should walk it?"

THIS PROPERTY IS CONDEMNED

Sam smiled slightly. "Last one to the bottom," he called out as he shoved off, "is the last one to the bottom."

As Tony hurried to catch up, he yelled, "Remember what happened the last time!"

"I know," Sam answered. He reached down and lightly tested his front and back hand brakes. Both grabbed like they were supposed to. "Come on," he shouted to the others.

This time he didn't grip the handlebars quite as hard as before. If anything jumped into his path, he was confident the bike could stop in time. Even the mailman would have been safe if he'd been on his route right now, but he wasn't.

At the bottom of the hill, all three bikes slid to a stop on the dirt drive in front of the Remmington Mansion. Dust swirled over them and continued blowing past the chain-link fence.

Tony stared through the fence. "You really wanna go in that place?"

Tyler's eyes blinked. "Looks kinda scary to me."

Sam's chest puffed out. "You chickens can stay here by the gate if you want to but I'm goin' in." He let his bike fall to the grass on the side of the dirt lane, walked through the gate and headed toward that big house.

"Don't you wanna hide your bike in the bushes?" Tyler asked.

Sam shook his head and didn't even bother to turn around. "Nope. I hope somebody steals it." His friends quickly rolled their bikes out of sight.

Sam continued walking down the dirt lane. He acted brave, but his heart pounded and his hands began to sweat.

33

"People have fences and gates for a reason," Tony complained as he ran to catch up.

Continuing to walk straight ahead, Sam said, "No one's forcing you to come along."

"I hate it when you say stuff like that."

Just to be safe, they left the dirt lane and walked through thick brush and trees. Sam picked up a long stick from the tall grass.

Tyler picked one up too. "Think we all need weapons?"

"It's to knock away the spider webs," Sam told him. "And if there are any animals in here."

Tyler and Tony stopped walking. "What kinda animals?" Tony asked.

Sam continued walking. "Bears, rattlesnakes, wildcats … you name it."

The others ran to catch up again. "Really?" Tyler asked.

Sam laughed. "Of course not. Now come on, follow me."

Tony spoke up next. "I read once that in places like Africa and India when they hunt dangerous wild animals, those guys make a great big circle. Then they start walking toward the center making all kinds of noise till they surround whatever it is they're trying to hunt."

Tyler lifted the stick he was holding above his head like a mighty sword. "I have a bad feeling about this."

"It's best we keep as quiet as possible," Sam told them, "'till we find out who or what's back here."

The deeper they went into the trees, the darker it got. The boys crept through the brush closer and closer toward that old, scary-looking house.

THIS PROPERTY IS CONDEMNED

Tyler only half whispered. "I really don't like this,"

Sam put a finger to his lips. "Shhh."

As the boys moved in closer toward the frightening mansion, Sam felt doubts that this was such a good idea. After the strange stories he'd heard, he thought anything could happen. *What if it's true about that person in the basement?*

Chapter 4

What Was That?

Even though the sun had been up for hours, no one would know it under the towering trees. Their branches, thick with leaves, blocked out most of the light giving the house an even more menacing look. The only sounds the boys heard came from cracking sticks under their feet, the occasional rustling of an animal in the brush, or birds sounding out their warnings.

"I don't think I like this," Tony complained. "Just think what this place must look like after dark."

Tyler stopped and gulped. "That's something I never wanna see in my lifetime."

The quivering feeling deep in Sam's stomach let him know he had to agree with his friends. But since they'd already made it this far, he decided to keep leading them forward.

When they came to a fallen tree, Sam motioned for his friends to hide with him behind it. The trunk was so big none of the boys could put his arms all the way around it.

Tony picked at some of the damp, rotted bark. "What makes a tree this big come down?"

"Probably just got old, gave up and died," Tyler said. "I wish I could have been here to see it fall."

Tony laughed. "How do you know it wouldn't have crashed right on your head?"

"Be quiet, you guys." Sam lifted up so he could see over the log. His friends did the same. From their position, they saw the house clearly now and it didn't help ease any fears.

Tony tapped Sam's shoulder. "What do you think?"

With a tremble in his voice, Tyler said, "I think we shouldn't have come back here."

Sam slowly shook his head. "It's worse than I thought."

"It does look bad," Tony said. "You sure somebody's in there?"

"You heard Mr. Kincaid."

"I know, but I'm starting to believe the people who say the place is haunted."

Sam did his best to sound confident. "Only one way to find out."

Tony let out a deep breath. "I hate it when you say things like that."

"Yeah," Tyler said. "It means we have to follow you no matter where you take us."

Sam's nervous eyes searched the huge house from top to bottom and side to side. He noticed broken windows, rotted boards on the porch, missing shutters, holes in the roof, and trash everywhere. Several large branches had fallen over the years and the grass had long since gone to weeds. He also noticed a garage that wasn't connected to the house. In it sat an old, rusted car. One of the crooked wooden garage doors still hung by only one hinge.

Tyler breathed a sigh. "At least they don't have a dog."

Tony looked at him. "Who says?"

"You hear any dogs?"

"Could be hiding in the basement just waiting for three stupid guys like us to come crawling up."

"Cut it out, Tony," Sam said. "It's bad enough being out here without having to worry about something like that."

"We should just be ready to run, that's all I'm sayin'."

"Have you ever tried to outrun a dog?" Tyler asked in disgust. "It can't be done."

Tony shuddered. "Now that *does* give me the creeps."

If they were ever to turn around and go back, now would have been the time. So far, it appeared no one knew the boys were there. For a couple of minutes, Sam thought about doing exactly that. *If there was an old lady inside that house and she needed help, what business is it of ours?*

Even though he felt fear and his heart continued pounding, Sam stood up, looked down to his friends and said, "Let's do this."

The others followed. The boys moved toward that scary house as silent as shadows. The only sounds came from breathing and the occasional rustling from thick leaves they shuffled through on the ground. A few feet ahead stood an iron fence with thick posts like hundreds of guards stretching clear around all four sides of the house.

"It really does look like something you'd see in a haunted house movie," Tony whispered. "And that fence is to keep people *out*, isn't it?"

Tyler stopped walking. "I'm so not liking this ... at all."

Sam tried to ignore them and kept moving forward. "Well, it's too late to turn back now."

"No, it's not," Tony said. "I could turn around and leave any time."

Sam motioned for them to follow, "Come on."

They walked along the tall iron fence toward a large gate. The fence stretched toward the sky, at least twice as tall as the boys, and seemed to dare anyone to try and get past it. At the top of each post stood a sharp, spear-like spike. The rough iron looked as if it might have been painted black at one time, but now only a rusty orange covered most of it.

Tony studied the ground. "I don't think many cars come back here."

"At least not very often," Sam said. He pointed to tire tracks in the sandy ruts on both sides of a weed-covered ridge in the center of the drive. Sam gave one of the massive gates a push and it began creaking open. Its spooky, screeching sound made all three boys shiver. Sam felt goose bumps on his arms and legs as he remembered all the haunted house stories he'd heard before.

Tony cleared his throat. "This isn't helping me not be scared,"

Just then the boys heard something else. "Look," Tyler said. "Someone's coming!"

THIS PROPERTY IS CONDEMNED

Like frightened birds, they dove into thick bushes near the drive. A pickup truck with two men inside drove up to the iron fence. One of the men jumped out and pushed the gates open wider as the truck moved through.

Sam read a name painted on the side of the truck, Hastings Development Corporation. "Where have I heard that name before?" he asked.

Tony kept watching the truck. "What name?"

"Hastings. I know that name."

"Sure you do," Tony said. "They practically built this whole town."

The boys watched from their hiding place as the truck pulled up to the front of the house and came to a stop. Both men stepped out, walked directly toward the house, climbed the steps and stopped at the front door. One of the men knocked a few times, but no one came out. So they moved off the porch and walked all the way around the mansion.

"What do you think they want?" Tyler asked in a whisper.

Sam shrugged his shoulders but said nothing. A few minutes later, the men came to the front of the house again, climbed back into their truck and drove away without closing the gates.

Tyler tugged on Sam's shirt sleeve. "Can we go now?"

"I told you nobody was inside that creepy house," Tony said.

Sam turned to him. "We don't know that for sure."

That made Tony gulp. "You're not still thinking of going up there, are you?"

"Didn't you say no one was inside? What's to be afraid of?"

Tony's wide eyes kept staring at the mansion. "Plenty! Just look at the place and tell me you don't think it's scary." His eyes darted around the area. "If we left right this minute, nobody would have to read about us in the paper tomorrow."

Tyler's head whipped over to Tony. "What's that supposed to mean?"

"I can see it now. Three boys found dead in the Remmington Mansion … in the *basement*!"

Tyler raised a clenched fist. "Tony, sometimes I think you fell out of one of those trees over there." He pointed toward the largest tree around, smiled and said, "Look, I can still see some of your relatives hanging from the branches."

"What are you tryin' to say?"

"That you're a nut and that's your family tree over there."

"Will you two cut it out," Sam whispered. He got to his feet and moved toward the open gates. Since those men had left them open, Sam walked right in. The others stuck close to him on either side.

Tony whispered first. "And the last time anyone saw the three helpless boys alive was when they walked through the gates of the old Remmington Mansion." Then he sighed.

Without any warning, they came to an abrupt stop when Sam held out both arms to block his friends from moving any further. "Shhh," he said as he raised a finger to his lips.

Tyler blinked and looked around. "What, where, who?"

"Didn't you see it?" Sam said.

Tony squeaked. "See what?"

"Something moved in that window to the right." He pointed. "Look. There it went again."

All three mouths dropped open as the curtains in that window quickly closed, but they didn't stop moving right away.

Tyler could hardly make the sounds come out of his mouth. "What in the …"

Tony tapped him on the shoulder. "You mean who in the world, don't you? I think it's the basement killer."

"Will you stop it!" Sam said. "All we have to do is walk up there, knock on the door and when no one opens it, we can go." He'd tried to sound brave, but is voice quivered and his knees seemed to almost rattle together as he forced his feet to move forward; one halting step after the other.

Tyler held on to Sam's right shirtsleeve while Tony clung to the other. Just as their feet reached the first rickety step, a fat, black crow called down to them from high up on the house somewhere. The boys nearly gave themselves whiplash as three heads shot backward. They spotted the crow as it leaped from a drainpipe and flew away.

"It's a warning," Tony said nearly crying.

Tyler shook his head. "No, it's a crow."

"Very funny."

Not one of the boys blinked his wide-open eyes, not even Tyler, from that first step, all the way to the front door. Sam wasn't sure if he had taken a breath either.

From the siding on the house, a doorbell switch dangled in the air, hanging by only one wire. *Bet it hasn't worked in years.*

Then he turned to see a rusty doorknocker made out of metal in the shape of a lion head. The lion's mouth stretched wide open, almost as if his job was to roar and eat anyone stupid enough to have come this far.

With trembling hands, Sam reached out to lift the lion's head and knock. But before he could do that, he heard the latch click from the inside. Hinges squeaked as the heavy, wooden door slowly … began … to … open!

Tyler moaned, "I don't feel so good."

Chapter 5

Enter at Your Own Risk

The front door of the old mansion creaked, its large, leaded glass window rattled and, as the door opened, the boys moved back.

Tony stepped a little too far back and his foot went through one of the rotted boards on the porch. Even as he fell backward, his eyes never moved from the door. "Hey, you guys," he whispered, "get me outta here."

Sam didn't turn around. Instead, he swallowed hard, took a deep breath and prepared for whatever it was on the other side of that door. What he saw next was not at all what he'd expected. Only a tiny woman stood in front of him. She wore a faded, flowery apron. Her white skin shimmered with wrinkles from a long life and her thin hair was even whiter than her skin. She peered over the top of a small pair of wire glasses. When she smiled, gaps showed a few missing teeth but Sam still noticed a kindness in her eyes.

In a scratchy, quiet voice she said, "If you're raising money for your club, I'd love to help you but I just don't have anything extra right now. I'm very sorry." That was followed by a little giggle as she tugged at her apron.

For the longest time, no one said a word. Then Tony begged, "Would somebody like to help get me out of here?"

Sam and Tyler turned to him. Sam had to pull a few small pieces of the broken, rotted wood out of the way before Tony's foot could be pulled back out.

"Goodness gracious," the little woman said in her soft voice. "I've been meaning to have that fixed." Her nervous eyes darted between the boys and the new hole in her porch floor.

Sam held up a few chunks of wood in his hand. "Looks like it's been this way for quite a while."

She sighed. "It's true. I just don't have the money I used to have to keep the place in good condition. My husband would be furious with me. When he was alive," she giggled again, "we certainly had all the money we needed." She looked off into the distance. "But I'm afraid he's gone now."

Tony looked out, too. "Where'd he go?"

She smiled and then in almost a giggle added, "Rudy ... I mean, Rudolph died a long time ago."

Tony snickered. "Your husband's name was Rudolph?" A broad smile came to his face and his mouth opened as he was about to say something else.

Tyler snapped his fingers and warned, "Don't even think about it."

"Yes," she said with a smile. She looked up and all around at the front of her gigantic house. "He built this grand old place. Rudy used to own the Remmington Sawmill before they stopped cutting trees around here. Every one of the boards in this very house came from his mill."

Sam turned to her. "Did you see those two men a few minutes ago?"

The old woman's expression changed to a look of fear. Her voice trembled, and her eyes closed slightly as she answered, "Mr. Hastings? I certainly did."

"Why didn't you come to the door?"

She folded her arms in defiance, squinted, pressed her lips tightly together and tapped the toe of one foot. "Do you know what that man wants to do?"

Sam shook his head.

"He wants to buy my house. The only problem is, where would I go?" She gazed out across the front porch, and her voice dropped softly. "This is my home."

Sam studied her troubled face. "Don't you have any family?"

A sense of sadness came to her eyes. She looked down and shook her head. "Not a soul."

"You mean you're all alone in this big house?" Tyler asked.

"That I am."

"Aren't you afraid?" Tony asked. "I would be."

She raised her head again with a sense of pride. "Sometimes. But I have a great big dog for protection."

"What'd I tell you guys?" Tony said with that familiar squeak. He moved back again and stepped right into the same hole. His eyes darted around the yard. "I *knew* she had a dog here someplace." Then he pulled his foot out.

"Would you like to meet my mean, ugly dog?"

"Nnn … no … not really," Sam said.

"Come inside, boys. I'll show you."

For some odd reason, Sam's imagination took a side road at that moment, which caused him to think about the story of Hansel and Gretel. *Great, and I didn't drop any white pebbles or breadcrumbs so somebody could follow our trail.* Then his mind jumped to a picture of himself standing, not in front of the Remmington Mansion but instead, in front of a cottage made of cakes and candy. *Wait a minute, didn't the lady in that story try to push the kids into her oven?* Like a distant voice in the forest, he began to hear his name.

"Hansel … Hansel … Samsel … *Sam!*

Sam blinked his eyes twice. Then he rubbed them.

Tony put a hand on his shoulder. "You all right?"

"She wants to show us her dog," Tyler added.

With caution, Sam, Tony, and Tyler walked into the massive entry of her house. Inside, Sam saw a giant chandelier hanging from a ceiling so high it hurt his neck to look all the way up there. The house gave off a musty odor. Since the trees blocked out so much light, it was difficult for the sun to reach any windows. Heavy, dark curtains covered those making the inside of the house look more like a dungeon.

Sam's voice quivered. "You don't have a big oven here, do you?"

The old woman chuckled. "Well, I do, but it hasn't worked in years. Now I use a smaller one." She stopped, turned around, and looked straight at Sam. "Did you want to see my oven?"

"N … no thanks."

The little woman shook her head. "Why was it you boys came out here?"

Sam let a nervous laugh escape. "Oh. I almost forgot. Do you know anything about that big sign out by the street?"

She put a hand to her chest. "Sign? What sign?"

"It says your property is dead," Tony told her.

Tyler shook his head. "Not dead,"

Sam interrupted. "It says your house is condemned,"

Now she clasped both hands together. "Condemned? Does it really say that?"

The boys slowly nodded together.

"Oh, dear." She gazed toward the front door. "So *that's* it." She stomped her foot on the hardwood floor. The sound sent a boom through the house like an echo in a deep, dark, dangerous cave.

"What's it?" Sam asked.

"Wait here. I'll be right back." The little old woman disappeared down a long, dark hallway and into one of the even darker rooms nearby.

Tony whispered without moving his lips. "I wouldn't go into a room that dark, no matter how much you paid me." He turned toward the front door. "Could we leave now?"

Tyler looked at him. "What for? She couldn't hurt anybody."

"But she said there's a dog."

"Have you seen one around here?" Sam asked. But even he looked for the nearest exit just in case some giant mongrel was to come storming out of the dark.

Tony's eyes also searched the huge cavernous room where they stood. He looked up the stairs and down again. Then his eyes stopped on the dark hallway as he pointed. "He could be hiding down there."

The woman hurried back to where the boys waited, but no dog followed her and she didn't have one on a leash.

Tony never took his eyes off her. "I thought you said you had a dog."

The woman shook her finger in the air. "That's right. I almost forgot." She shuffled over to a table under a window where the boys had first seen the curtain move. She reached out, turned the switch on an old boom box and pushed a button. Then, in an almost evil witch's voice, she cackled, "Here kitty, kitty, kitty."

No sooner had she spoken those strange words than the room filled with the echoing sounds of the most ferocious, slobbering dog any of the boys had ever heard. Its vicious barking sent cold chills from the bottom of Sam's feet all the way to the top of his head and back down again. It made Mr. Kincaid's watchdog seem like nothing more than a harmless stuffed toy. His barking made Sam think the oven might be a better way to go.

Tony grinned and said with a laugh, "Every mailman in Harper's Inlet just dropped their mail and ran for their lives."

Then she turned the sound off and looked at the boys with a sly grin. "That's my dog."

"Ever have to use it?" Sam asked.

"Not so much anymore. Most people have stopped bothering me. That is until those mean Hastings men started coming around. At first, it seemed to scare them but I think they caught on that I don't really *have* a dog."

Tony fiddled with his shirt collar. "Boy, am I ever glad to hear that."

The woman held papers in her hand that she'd brought from the dark room. "Come and look at these." She pushed a few yellowed newspapers and ragged magazines out of the way and spread her papers onto a dark, round wooden table with a tall lamp in the center. "What do you make of these?"

Sam took a few minutes to pick up several of the papers and read over what they said. When he finished, he looked to her and asked, "Do you know what these are?"

She shook her head and touched a finger to the side of her glasses. "My eyes aren't what they used to be."

He held up one of the papers from the pile. "This one is from the City Council. It says if you don't fix up your house, they can take it away from you and knock it down."

"Oh, my," she whimpered, stumbled backward and almost didn't make it to a chair before falling. "Oh, dear. Whatever shall I do?" Her short gasps for breath made Sam worry.

"There's a list of things here. Want me to read it?"

She put a hand up to her neck and nodded.

"Let's see," he began, "the roof needs to be replaced, your wiring is shot, the paint's coming off. You've got a lot of broken windows, there are rotted boards, the yard's a wreck ... it goes on for three pages."

Tony looked down at his foot. "Yeah, I already found out about the rotten boards."

Tears welled up in the woman's eyes and flowed down her wrinkled cheeks. She shook her head. "This is terrible, just terrible. I don't have the money to do any of those things." Her chest heaved as she struggled for several more short breaths.

Sam tried to use his most comforting voice. "But if you could get them all fixed, you think you'd want to stay in this house?"

Her face brightened and her voice became stronger. "Certainly! There's only one way they're taking me out of this place. The same way Rudy went."

Tony looked to the door again. "What way was that?"

"In a hearse."

That made him shudder. "Did it have anything to do with the basement?"

She sat up a little straighter. "How did you know that?"

Now it was Tyler who barely moved his lips. "Could we please go now?"

But Sam walked over, put his hand on Mrs. Remmington's shoulder and asked, "Would it be okay if I keep these for a few days?"

She stared at the papers in his hand and slowly shook her head. "I don't know."

He smiled. "I'll bring them back. I promise."

"Well …" she said, "I suppose that would be all right."

"Come on, you guys."

His friends beat him to the front door. Tyler streaked through first. "I thought you'd never ask."

THIS PROPERTY IS CONDEMNED

Sam called back to Mrs. Remmington. "We'll be back."

Tony grinned. "And don't forget to feed that dog."

She smiled slightly, but her tears didn't stop falling. Back out on the porch, Sam shut the door behind them.

With a confused look, Tyler asked, "How come you wanted those papers?"

Sam smiled and held them up like an attorney who knew he could win his toughest case with the evidence. "Because I've got an idea."

"Oh, no," Tony said as he put his hands up toward Sam. "I know what happens when you get that look in your eye."

Sam motioned for his friends to follow. "Come on. We gotta hurry." They jumped off the porch steps and ran toward their bikes.

Chapter 6

Terrible Discovery

The boys quickly reached their bikes at the end of the lane. Sam rolled up the pages Mrs. Remmington had given him like a small newspaper, jammed them into the top of his jeans and hopped on his bike.

"What now?" Tyler asked.

Sam began peddling toward the street. "We can't let her lose that house."

"But how?"

"I'm not sure yet. All I know is we've got to do something."

Tony looked up toward the sky and sighed. "Great news."

The boys hurried off toward Sam's house. They had to push their bikes up Landon Hill Road since none of them owned one with the right gears to peddle to the top of such a steep climb.

"Just once I'd like to have a racing bike that could make this hill," Sam told his friends. Together they huffed, puffed and grunted all the way to the top. Then they jumped onto their bikes and raced off again.

The boys peddled so fast, they could almost have been mistaken for professional racers. Well, no one would have made that mistake by looking at what Sam was riding. Back at his house, Sam dropped his bike into the grass. As soon as his feet hit the dirt, he started running for the back door, up the steps, through the door, and to his room. Tony and Tyler followed right behind him. When they reached Sam's bedroom, he spread the papers out over his bed. All three guys were nearly out of breath.

Tyler fought for each gasp of air. "What do you expect to find in there?" Then he picked up one of the papers.

Sam struggled to breathe just as much as the others. "Information."

Tony collapsed onto the end of Sam's bed. "What kind of information?"

"Well, we already know Hastings Development is involved somehow. All we gotta do is find out where they fit in."

Tony reached for a paper. "I've seen some trucks around here that say Hastings Construction on the side."

Sam didn't look up. "Probably the same company." For the next several minutes, Sam studied each paper in silence.

It didn't take long before Tyler and Tony got bored. After catching their breath again, they walked over to play video games. Sam continued going through Mrs. Remmington's papers, carefully reading each one. Then he stopped on one when his eyes caught those words again. *Your property will be condemned.* He continued reading silently. *You have ninety days to bring the structure up to code.* He bit his bottom lip and shook his head. Next he found the three-page list again with all of the things that needed fixing. Then he studied the dates on the different notices and forms. *These papers are almost two months old.*

Tyler complained. "Stop cheating."

"Do over!" Tony yelled.

"No do-overs. When your guy falls off the cliff, he's dead … then it's my turn."

"To fall off the cliff?"

Tyler slammed his control down. "You know what I mean."

"Oh, you'll be going off the cliff all right."

"Just take your turn."

Sam heard them in the background. They could just as well have been in another room because he couldn't help concentrating on the words he'd found. Finally, he said out loud. "They're gonna take the place away from her."

Tyler turned from the video game screen and asked, "Who is?"

"It doesn't really say who, only that's what they're planning to do."

"But why?" Tony asked.

Sam rolled off of his bed and stood up. "Let's go down to the courthouse."

"What for?" Tony complained, "I'm winning."

Tyler just frowned back at him.

"I want to check out something."

"You just heard that I was winning, that's why."

Tyler sent a blast of air out of his nearly closed lips. "Nobody cares who's winning,"

"You sure do."

Sam put his hands on his hips and gave his friends one of those looks. "Come on, you guys. Let's go. If I'm right about this, she doesn't have much time."

"Time for what?" Tony asked.

Tyler's voice went up a little higher. "Is Mrs. Remmington gonna die?"

Sam shook his head. "She doesn't have much time to fix up the old place."

The boys bolted out the door, thundered down the hall, hit the back door and climbed on their bikes. If there were a speed limit for bike riders in Harper's Inlet, all three of these guys would get a ticket for sure.

They were already halfway down the first block when Tyler asked, "Who we goin' to see?"

"Since my dad's a scientist, he already knows a lot of government people here."

"So?"

"These guys come over for dinner and stuff. That's when I meet all of them. They keep telling me, 'If there's anything we can ever do for you, you just let us know.'"

"Why's that?" Tony asked.

"Come on," Tyler said. "You know our friend *Sammy* here. People from Marshfield probably called ahead to tell 'em how famous he is."

The boys leaned into the next corner. Tony pulled up alongside Tyler. "You really think so?"

"Sure I do. He's practically a legend, and he's not even in high school yet."

"I guess my dad's told them stories about some of the projects."

"So who's your next victim?" Tony joked as he pulled his bike up alongside of Sam.

Even with his pitiful bike, Sam pulled into the lead again. "A guy in the county clerk's office."

They rocketed to the next corner and turned onto Main Street.

Tyler started straining for breath. "What can *he* tell us?"

"That's where they keep all the records."

"I thought we just had CD's and files now," Tony said.

Sam laughed. "Not *records* records. I mean records."

"Huh?"

Sam threw his head back and laughed even harder as he called out. "Tony, sometimes I think you do things like that on purpose."

"Honest, I don't know *what* you're talking about." He pulled his bike up next to Sam's again.

"Records. It's another name for lists."

"How do those help us?"

"It should show who's trying to smash her house down and why."

After another block-and-a-half, the boys skidded to a stop in front of the county courthouse. Without even stopping to lock them, they jammed their bikes into a rack and hurried inside.

"Sam!" a man called out right away from the far end of the hallway.

Tyler slowed down. "Are we in trouble already?" he asked.

Tony whispered. "What'd you do now?"

"Nothing. I know him. That's one of my Dad's friends I told you about."

Tony glanced around in fear. "I don't like for anyone in a building like this to know a thing about me."

"It's not a jail," Tyler told him.

"No," Sam said, "that's on the other side."

Tony came to an abrupt stop and grabbed Sam's arm, spinning him completely around. "It is?"

"Sure. You live here and don't even know that?"

Tony only shook his head.

By the time Sam turned back around, the man had reached where they were standing. "What brings you boys down here today?"

Tony answered with a quiver in his voice. "Our bikes?"

"You're a funny kid," the man said.

"This is Mr. Thomas," Sam told them.

"That's right. Ed Thomas is my name." He turned to Sam. "Now what can I do for you?"

Sam pulled the roll of the papers from his jeans and gave the top sheet to Mr. Thomas. "We need to find out more on the house they talk about here." He pointed to a line toward the top of the form.

A pair of glasses hung by a strap from Mr. Thomas' neck. He reached down, slipped them on and held the paper close. After reading some of the information, he looked up. "Come on into my office. I'll see what we can do." He motioned for the boys to follow, then opened a door with wood on the bottom and glass at the top. Letters on the glass said County Clerk. Inside the boys noticed several people standing in lines as people on the other side of the counter helped them.

Tony looked at one line and asked out loud. "Do we have to wait with all those people?"

Several of them turned to see who'd said that.

Mr. Thomas put a hand to his mouth, cleared his throat and motioned to one of the people behind the counter. Sam heard a buzzing sound and Mr. Thomas pushed open another door. "Right this way," he said to the boys.

Tony turned and looked at the people still waiting in line, smiled and whispered, "Makes a guy feel kinda important, doesn't it?"

"Will you get in there before they all try to come in behind us?" Tyler grumbled.

They walked over to the front of a large, dark wooden desk. Mr. Thomas moved around to the other side, sat in a heavy, wooden chair, held out his hand and said, "Show me what else you've got."

Sam unrolled the papers and spread them out across the top of the desk. "What're these about?"

The boys waited as Mr. Thomas read through several of the papers. Occasionally he nodded his head, without looking up, and simply grunted or said, "Uh-huh." One time he said, "That's not good." And another time he stopped reading and said, "Humm." When he'd finally finished, he slowly took off his glasses, rubbed his eyes, held up one of the papers and looked to Sam. "According to this, the property is about to be condemned."

Sam let out a disgusted breath. "We already know that. There's a sign out in front of her house right now."

Mr. Thomas looked down at the papers on his desk. "Not for long." He picked another one of them up and held it in his hand.

"What do you mean?"

"Says here there's going to be a four-lane highway running right through the middle of her living room."

Tony's eyes widened and his eyebrows went up. "How's that gonna work?" he asked as he scratched his head. "She could be going from the kitchen to the dining room and get run over by a garbage truck right in her own house."

Tyler laughed at him. "Like that old video game you still love to play."

Mr. Thomas smiled. "You don't understand."

"I sure don't," Tony said. "Who puts a road through the middle of their own house?"

Tyler nodded and his eyes got bigger. "Oh, I get it. The house won't be there anymore, right?"

Tony sank down into a chair, shaking his head. "First you tell me a road's going through her house. Then you say the house won't be there. Why don't you guys make up your minds?"

Mr. Thomas looked to him. "It's pretty simple. Early on, she gets a warning. If she ignores the warning, she gets a second and a third. If she ignores those and fails to make the needed repairs, that's when the trouble begins. Even when people have gone out there to visit her and let her know what's happening, she'd never come to the door. Some of them reported being scared off by her big dog."

Tyler put a hand over his mouth to cover his snicker.

Sam let out another deep breath. "How many more months does she have?"

Mr. Thomas looked as if he didn't understand Sam's question. "Months? She only has weeks."

Tyler nearly shouted. "Weeks?"

"After that, the house has to come down."

Sam turned to leave. He called back to Mr. Thomas, "Thanks for your help."

Out in the hallway, he stopped his friends. "We can't let this happen."

Tony gave him a strange look. "What?"

"No matter what it takes, we gotta help that old lady keep her house."

"Why?" Tony asked. "So she can have cars driving through the middle of it?"

Sam shook his head. "That's *not* gonna happen."

Tyler looked up toward the high ceiling in the hallway. "Here he goes again."

Chapter 7

Sam's Big Plan

After the boys walked down the courthouse steps and reached their bikes, Tony asked, "How come *we* gotta be the ones to do this?"

"I don't know," Sam said with a smile. "I just can't help myself."

"But that means we have to *not* be able to help it too."

Sam continued smiling. "I know, and that's what makes us such good friends."

"It'll make us a lot of extra work if you ask me."

"Well, nobody did," Tyler said.

"Let's get together again tomorrow," Sam told his friends.

"What are you gonna do?" Tony asked.

"I have another idea."

"Work, work, work … that's all we do."

Max Elliott Anderson

Sam hurried off on his bike. As he rode through town, he couldn't help thinking about some of the other projects he'd worked so hard to organize in other places. He remembered the park where, because of his help, children enjoyed new playground equipment, older people found freshly painted benches, and dogs now romped in their own section of the park. In one town where he used to live, it would have been hard not to notice the planters and large trash cans Sam had raised money to buy. He especially enjoyed thinking about the antique-looking street lamps on both sides of the main street. That's right; Sam was responsible for those, too.

He coasted to a stop in his back yard, dropped his bike to the ground in its usual place and ran to his computer. First he looked for information about condemned property. His browser brought up over eight hundred thousand entries on the subject. Sam slumped back in his chair and rubbed his forehead. "This could take longer than I thought." His search turned up information such as how to know if your property has been condemned, reasons for condemning property, and a whole lot more.

After searching for a several minutes, his eyes stopped on a headline that read, "Greedy developers can take your property … legally!" He opened that one and began reading. "Condemning property has become a tool that serves the interests of greedy developers."

Sam scratched the side of his head. *What does that mean?* He read a little farther and found the words "eminent domain." When he looked that up, he found it meant the government has the right to take private property for public use. Then he read news stories about people who had lost their homes because their communities wanted the land for other development. But even after the homes were taken and the people had to move away, some of those towns never built anything new on the land. He looked around his room. *Could people in Harper's Inlet just take away this house if they wanted it?* He read about how the homeowners are paid for their houses but, still, it didn't seem right to him.

When he heard his dad come home, Sam hurried out to see him. "Dad. Do you know what eminent domain is?"

His father hung his jacket on a hook next to the door. "Sure I do. Sometimes officers from the sheriff's department have to take papers to people about that."

Sam pulled a paper from his pocket. "Like this one?"

His father took the paper, read the first few lines and looked up. "Where'd you get this?"

"From the sweetest, little old lady you ever saw."

"You mean Mrs. Remmington?"

Sam's eyes widened. "You know her?"

"I've heard of her. How do you know this woman?" His father continued reading silently from the form.

"We went to her house. Did you know they're trying to knock it down?"

His father nodded but didn't look up. "She hasn't kept the place up from what I hear, but I really don't know much about it. And this paper says she's running out of time."

Sam let out a long sigh. "I know. How can someone come in and just flatten it?"

"There are rules here. All counties have them. If people don't live up to the rules, bad things can happen."

"But if she did fix it up … could she stay in her house?"

His father looked up again. "Probably. I don't see why she couldn't." Then he shook his head. "But there might not be enough time."

Sam grabbed the paper from his father's hand, turned and dashed toward his room again. "Thanks, Dad."

"And thanks for the paper cut," his father said as he put a finger to his mouth.

Back at his computer, Sam continued reading out loud, "The county road commission wanted to build a road. There was a little old widow lady whose house was standing right in the way."

Just like Mrs. Remmington.

"In the end, the county got what it wanted. The woman had to sell out and move away."

"But our little old widow lady'll never move," he said out loud. "Not if I can help it!" Then he called Tyler.

"Hello."

"Hey, Tyler. I've been doing a little research about the old house and all."

"Find anything interesting?"

"Yeah. They can take it away from her all right if she doesn't get it fixed up."

"Really? People can do that?"

"Uh-huh. So here's the plan." He went on to detail what he and Tony were about to do. And in typical Sam Cooper fashion, the plan was too big, the costs were too high, and the time was entirely too short. Nothing new here so far.

After he hung up, Sam spun in his chair back to the computer. In his search, he stumbled across an organization that helped people keep their land, houses, and businesses from being taken over by their local, county, or state government. He saved that in his favorites file. Just as he finished, his mother called him for supper.

At the table Sam asked, "So, Dad. You said if Mrs. Remmington fixed up everything then maybe she could stay there, right?"

"What's this about, and who's Mrs. Remmington?" his mother asked as she passed a dish.

"Somebody's trying to knock down her house."

"How terrible."

"It's not that simple," his father said. "According to papers Sam brought home, she has a lot of things to fix on her old mansion. I don't think she has the money and, from one of the papers Sam showed me, she doesn't have the time either."

Sam looked around the room where they sat. "But what if we had a bunch of stuff to fix on this house?" he asked with a sad voice. "Could they make us move, too?"

His father sat up straight in his chair and held his knife and fork like weapons. "I wouldn't let that happen."

"How could you stop 'em?"

"I'd make sure to fix everything on the list so they'd *have* to leave us alone."

"They would?"

His father nodded.

"But I read online today that government people can take land and houses away just because they think there's a better use for it that'll help more people."

"What a terrible thing," his mother said.

After rushing to finish, like he was a contestant in the annual hotdog-eating contest, Sam asked, "Could I be excused?" He didn't mean to, but that question was instantly followed by a thunderous belch. He covered his mouth and snickered, "Sorry."

His mother flashed a disapproving smile. "You mean excused for what you just did and before any chocolate cake?"

Those last two magic words instantly made his mouth water, but he had more important things on his mind. Sam was on a mission. He nodded, then shook his head.

"Well, which is it?" she asked.

"I have something to do."

His father stared at him. "Must be pretty important."

Sam squirmed in his chair. "It is."

After being excused and turning his back on a soft, sweet, chocolate cake with extra thick frosting, he raced back to his computer. With a graphics program, he began designing small posters that he and his friends could pass out on the street. They said things like, "You can make a difference," and "Mrs. Remmington needs your help."

While he printed them out on bright yellow paper left over from an old school assignment, Tony called. "What's the work project this time?"

"How'd you know there'd be one?"

"Because this is what you said you do and because Tyler called to warn me. He said I'd better start working on my excuse if I ever expected to get out of it."

"But don't you think it's worth it?"

"Seems like you think that about every one of the projects you've done."

"I do, don't I."

"Just once, I wish you'd MYOB," Tony said with a sigh.

"MYOB?"

Tony laughed into the phone. "You know, mind your own business."

"But what if she was your grandmother or it was your *own* house? What then?"

"You really know how to hurt a guy. I love my Grammy."

"Well, then?"

Tony sighed again. "Okay. Where and when?"

"Call Tyler back. Tell him to meet us in front of the hardware store around nine tomorrow morning."

"What for?"

"Just be there."

"Oh, all right, we will."

That night Sam went to bed with a big smile on his face. *If everything works the way I think it will, we can save her house.* In the morning, he ate a quick breakfast and shot out the door before nine.

"I'm surprised to see you guys are on time," he said to his friends as his bike coasted to a stop in front of Tyler and Tony.

"What do you mean ... on time?" Tony said. "We beat *you* here."

"Let's get started," Sam told them.

"Started on what?" Tony asked.

Tyler laughed. "He didn't tell you?"

Tony shook his head. "Neither did you. Probably knew I wouldn't show up if you did."

Sam pushed his bike to a rack and the others followed. After locking them, he said, "We're going to walk up and down the street, hollering as loud as we can, and pass these out." He pulled copies of the bright, yellow posters from an old, ragged newspaper delivery bag that hung around his neck. Each of his friends took a stack of them.

Tony read the poster and asked, "What good's this gonna do?"

A bright morning sun hit Sam's face as he stared off into the distance. "By the time we're finished, we'll have that old house looking like new. Then no one would dare try to touch it."

Chapter 8

Nobody's Gonna Stop Us

Tyler looked up from the yellow papers in his hands. "We should just use your metal detector, find some gold or something and that old lady's troubles would be over."

Sam and his friends each held a stack of posters. Tyler and Tony crossed the street while Sam stayed where he was. Then they walked down the sidewalks yelling as they went.

Sam called out. "Help save the Remmington Mansion,"

From his side of the street, Tyler echoed. "You can help. Don't let 'em knock the place down,"

Tony didn't say much. He just passed out his posters to people walking along. This went on until they had covered most of the main streets in town. About an hour and a half later, they met back at the corner of Main Street and Ocean View.

Tony looked around to see if anyone was staring at him. "I hate the way people look at you when you're doing something like this. They think you're crazy or something."

Tyler wiped his nose. "Didn't bother me. What's next?"

Sam looked at the posters his friends still had left in their hands and pulled the last few out of his bag. "Let's take the rest of these and see if some of the stores will let us put 'em up in their windows."

Tyler's face brightened. "That's a great idea."

"Yeah," Tony said, "no more yelling on the street."

Tyler laughed. "Like you did any."

Sam looked up the street. "I think it would be harder for the stores to turn us down if we stick together."

Tony started walking. "I hate doing this by myself anyway. Let's go."

Their first stop was at the hardware store. Before asking about the posters, Sam bought a roll of sticky tape. The manager let them put up two posters because his store had two different entrance, and since Sam bought his own tape there.

Once they were out the door, Sam turned to Tony. "That wasn't so bad, now, was it?"

"Not as long as we're together."

The boys continued delivering posters to stores, shops, a coin laundry, fast-food restaurants, gas stations, and anywhere the owners would let them put up a poster.

After most of them were gone, Sam said, "I'm surprised so many let us do that."

Later, Tyler sat on the edge of one of the plant boxes built to beautify their streets. "That's the way this town is gonna be from now on," he said. "When they know Sam Cooper has a project, who could stand in the way?"

Sam smiled. "Yeah. I guess it *is* true." But again, he felt that same old uncomfortable tightness down deep in his stomach.

Tony straightened the few posters he still held in his hands. "I think a store'd be scared not to do what you tell them."

Sam gave him a disapproving look. "I don't tell them. I ask."

"I know, but who wants to be the one and only store in Harper's Inlet that doesn't have a poster."

"Yeah," Tyler said. "They couldn't afford the business they'd lose. Even your dad let us put some up around the marina."

Off they hurried to get rid of the rest of their posters. As they turned the corner onto Palm Street, Sam held out his arms and stopped his friends. He pointed to one of the Hastings Construction trucks sitting against the curb.

The boys began walking again when Tyler noticed something. "Hey. I think that guy's taking pictures of us."

"Really?" Tony said. Then he began making all kinds of goofy faces and jumping around like a gorilla. He stuck fingers in both sides of his mouth and pulled on his cheeks. With two other fingers, he pulled down the skin at the bottom of his eyes and stuck his tongue out. Then he moved it from side to side while continuing to grunt.

"Stop it," Sam scolded, but it was too late. One of the men stepped out of the truck, blocking the boys' path.

Tony stood up straight again and moved in closer to Sam.

Tyler whispered. "Now you did it."

"Just wanted to give them something to look at," Tony whispered back.

The man put out his hand. "What do you boys have there?"

"Nothing," Tony told him and quickly slipped the posters behind his back.

"Oh, I don't know. Maybe we'd like to put some of those up in our office."

Tony nodded. "Sure you would."

"Shhh!" Sam warned.

"Might even want to donate a little money, too."

Sam waved a finger. "No, that's all right."

Then the second man climbed out of the truck. He looked even bigger than the first. Sam felt an uneasy quiver quickly roll through his stomach. And it made him breathe a little faster.

Then the first man demanded, "Give them to us." Both men grabbed for the posters, but the boys wouldn't let go. Suddenly, the small stack Sam clung to tore in half sending pieces of bright yellow paper sailing high into the air.

"You're too late anyway," Tyler told them. "These things are all over town now."

A loud voice behind them demanded, "What's going on there?"

Sam looked back to see a police officer stepping out of his patrol car. The men moved back while torn papers continued drifting to the sidewalk like confetti at a parade.

"Uh," one of the men stammered, "we ... um ... ya know ... we was just tryin' ta help these kids here put up some of their posters."

Tony looked toward the sky. "Put them up in the air you mean ... and in a bunch of pieces too."

76

"I could cite you for littering," the officer threatened. He picked up one of the torn papers. "And probably destruction of property, too.""It's okay," Sam said in a nervous voice. "I think they were just leaving. And we can pick everything up."

"You sure?"

"I'm sure." Sam and his friends leaned down to gather all the torn papers, while the men hurried back to their truck, climbed in and drove away.

"What was that all about, Sam?" the officer asked.

Sam threw his pieces into one of the large sidewalk trash cans. Then he wiped his hands on his pants. "I think those guys have something to do with trying to tear down the Remmington Mansion. They don't want us to help that old lady fix it up."

"Why not?"

"I'm working on that part."

"Well, you boys be careful."

"We will. But if you could have seen her face, you'd want to help too."

"Sounds like a fine thing you're doing, boys. Let me know if there's anything more I can do."

With a big smile, Tony watched the truck drive away. "You just did."

The officer hurried back to his patrol car and drove in the same direction the truck had gone. Sam and his friends watched while the driver of the truck made sure to stay under the speed limit.

Tyler turned to Sam. "Is that it?"

"Yeah," Tony added, "can we be done now?"

Sam shook his head. "No. Now comes the hard part."

Tony flashed a quizzical look. "Hard part! It was embarrassing enough walking up and down the street yelling at people."

Tyler turned to him. "Yelling? I don't think I heard you say two words the whole time."

"Maybe not, but you guys were yelling and everybody knows we're best friends. It made me feel like an idiot."

Tyler punched him on the arm. "That's because you *are* an idiot."

"We have to go back to stores and building places next," Sam said.

Tony rubbed on the spot where Tyler had hit him. "What for? They already have our posters up."

"I know. Now we have to find all the stuff we need to fix the Remmington house."

Tony took two steps backward. He should have looked first because he fell right into a big cement flower planter. "You're not serious," he said.

"Sure, I am."

"You mean you think us kids can do all that work?" He put one hand over the other and spread them as far apart as he could reach. "The place is three stories high. We could break our necks."

"We know *you* could," Tyler joked.

Sam watched Tony pull himself back out of the planter. "We're going to ask other people to help with the work."

"Like who?" Tyler asked.

"Painters, builders, landscaping guys ... whoever, wherever, and whatever we need."

THIS PROPERTY IS CONDEMNED

"Now I get it," Tony said as he brushed dirt from his jeans.

"Where you wanna go first?" Tyler asked.

"Let's start with the biggest place for the biggest job."

"Where's that?"

"The building supply center."

"Yeah," Tony said. He held up both hands and wiggled his fingers in the air. "I can't wait to see you use your *magic* powers."

"I don't have any magic powers."

"Are you kidding?" Tony said. "Remember telling us about the time you wanted Marshfield to break the record for planting new trees?"

"That was the funniest thing I ever heard," Tyler said. "You had people all over that town digging holes in the ground."

Sam stood up a little straighter. "And the trees still look nice there."

"Or the time you got everybody to write the governor so they could build onto the old library."

"I know," Tyler said. "And don't forget, that place has a day named after you. You're the town hero."

Sam shook his head. "I am not. I'm a kid just like you."

Tony shook his head. "You're nothing like us and we all know it."

"Come on," Sam said. "Let's go. If we can get Mr. Grinwall to give us the materials, then this project will get done for sure."

As they rode their bikes toward the building supply center, Sam thought, *what if he won't give us what we need?*

Chapter 9

An Impossible Request

Sam felt that uneasy feeling in his stomach again as they rode into the parking lot of the building center. It looked much bigger to him today for some reason. And what if they didn't want to help on the project?

Tyler whistled. "Look at all those cars."

"They must make millions here," Tony added.

Sam felt a lump in his throat as they walked through the automatic glass doors. *Looks bigger inside than before, too.*

Right away Mr. Grinwall spotted them. He quickly walked toward the boys with a smile.

That's a good sign.

"Okay … okay, everybody's talking about your project. What's it going to cost me?" Mr. Grinwall reached for his wallet.

Sam held up his hands toward the store owner and shook his head. "Could we go to your office and talk?"

The man held his wallet in one hand. "Does this project call for my checkbook?"

Sam shook his head again.

"Uh-oh. Sounds serious. All right then, right this way."

Sam swallowed hard. "It is serious,"

Mr. Grinwall led the boys to a metal stairway that went up to the store's offices. People worked at desks and computers in each office the boys walked past. It looked to Sam like some of them had meetings with salesmen because of the samples on a couple desks.

"This might be the most serious project ever," Sam told Mr. Grinwall as he sank into one of the chairs in his office. Tyler and Tony sat together on a couch against another wall in the room. Anyone who knew Sam knew it was best to let him do all the talking.

Sam fidgeted in his chair, not quite sure where to start.

"What are we talking about here?" Mr. Grinwall asked. He opened a large, black company checkbook and took out his pen. "A hundred? Five hundred? What?"

Sam didn't speak.

"My goodness. You're not looking for a *thousand*, are you?"

Sam shook his head and looked toward the floor. "It isn't money we need most."

Mr. Grinwall sat back and relaxed into his big, brown, leather chair. "That's a relief." He closed the cover of the checkbook again.

Forgetting some of his own fundraising disasters of the past, Tony blurted out, "Wait till you hear what we really need."

THIS PROPERTY IS CONDEMNED

Sam first looked to his friend, turned back and pulled one of the last posters out of his pocket. He pointed to the first line. "What we need is to help Mrs. Remmington get her house fixed up again …a nd fast."

Mr. Grinwall took the poster and studied it for a moment. Then he placed it on his desk. "But I don't understand, why the hurry?"

"If we don't, it's gonna be condemned."

Mr. Grinwall sat up straight in his chair. "Really?"

With a sad face, Sam nodded. "Yes, sir. Somebody wants to tear it down if she doesn't make all kinds of repairs."

By now Tyler sounded a little braver. "Yeah, and put a road right through the middle of her living room."

"But who? Who wants to tear it down?"

"I think it's Hastings Construction."

Without any warning, Mr. Grinwall pounded a fist on his desk. The sound made the boys jump. "Hastings? I'd love a chance to get even with those guys."

Tony sat forward. "How come?"

Mr. Grinwall looked out a window in his office, almost as if Sam and his friends weren't even there. In a lower, quieter voice he said, "Nothing … I mean it's personal." He turned back to Sam. "It's just we've got a disagreement that goes back a few years."

The boys continued listening.

"Let's just say the deal cost me a bundle." Then a strange smile spread across the man's face. "So, what can I do for you?"

Sam's eyes widened and he felt relieved. "You mean you'll help us?"

"Anything you need."

Then Tony did it again. "Maybe you'd better hear more about it before you say that."

Sam kept his eyes on Mr. Grinwall. "Anything?" he asked.

Mr. Grinwall nodded with a smile. So Sam pulled another paper from his pocket. "I made a list of the things we'd need from your store."

Mr. Grinwall took the list, gave it a quick glance and looked up to Sam. "Pretty confident, aren't you?"

Sam certainly hadn't felt very confident.

After Mr. Grinwall finished reading the list, he slumped back into his chair, whistled, and looked up at Sam. "Do you have any idea how much all of these things cost?"

He shook his head. "No, sir ... no idea at all."

"Well, I can tell you it's thousands and tens of thousands."

At first Sam gulped. "But that old house is a part of this town's history. We can't let anybody knock it down."

Mr. Grinwall smiled. "Especially Hastings, right?" He rubbed both sides of his chin for a moment.

Sam felt those doubts creeping in, and a tight feeling in his stomach started up all over.

"Tell you what," Mr. Grinwall said. "Why don't you boys give me a day or two to think about it? Maybe we can come up with something."

Sam's face beamed. "You mean it?"

"I sure do. Might even let some of my guys help out on the project."

"Thank you," Sam said as he stood to leave. "But hurry, would you? We don't have much time."

Mr. Grinwall stood and reached out to shake Sam's hand. "You're really something Sam Cooper. When you grow up, you should run for mayor of Harper's Inlet one day; maybe even governor."

Even though Sam smiled back, he swallowed hard. Then he and his friends left the office and raced down the stairs feeling more confident, now that they could find everything they would need for Mrs. Remmington's extreme major mansion makeover.

By the end of the day, the boys had lined up all the building materials they needed, if Mr. Grinwall came through, as well as the paint, electrical, landscaping, and brick repair. Owners from other shops and stores had also suggested they could probably find some of the people who would be needed to help with the work.

Tony couldn't hold back his smile. "It's fun being your friend. It almost makes me feel famous or something."

"Let's go back out to the mansion tomorrow," Sam said. "I want to give Mrs. Remmington the good news."

"What do we do now?" Tyler asked.

"I don't know about you guys, but I promised to mow the grass this afternoon. That is if my dad has our old, tired lawnmower put back together."

Tyler snapped his fingers. "Shoot, I almost forgot. I have to do that too."

Tony laughed. "You mean put your lawnmower together or the two of you are gonna mow Sam's lawn?"

They both gave him a pained look.

"Just kidding, guys, just kidding. Think I'll go home and feed my guppies."

"Be careful you don't fall in," Tyler teased.

"That's not funny. I can't help it I fall sometimes. My mom says I'm growing too fast again."

"Better not let it happen around any *girls*," Tyler said. "Wouldn't want you to fall in *love* or anything."

Tony's face turned three shades of red. "Man, I hope that never happens."

"I'll see you guys later," Sam told them as he peddled away toward home. When he got there, he noticed his father's car in the driveway. *Strange*, he thought. Then he found him in the garage.

"Hey, Dad, whatcha doing home in the middle of the day?"

"I took a break so I could pick up a few lawnmower parts for this thing. Just got finished putting her back together."

Sam looked toward the sky. "Great. You have no idea how happy that makes me feel."

His father wiped his hands on a rag. Then he leaned down, took the starter rope in one hand and held the mower handle with the other. He gave one mighty pull … and …*nothing* happened.

The frown on Sam's face turned to a slight smile.

Then his father moved the throttle to a different position and gave a second pull. That's when the motor sputtered, coughed, wheezed, and quickly filled the garage with thick, blue smoke.

Sam choked inside the cloud. "You fixin' the mower, or just fixin' to kill us?"

THIS PROPERTY IS CONDEMNED

His father shut it off again. "There. She's good as new."

Just once I wish we really would get something new.

"I gotta get back to some paperwork. See you later."

"Bye, Dad."

Sam had only finished about half of the yard when something strange happened. A truck that looked like the same one from Hastings Construction with the men who had tried to take away his posters drove down his street. When it reached Sam's house, they stopped for a moment, the man took a long look at his house and then the truck sped away.

"If you're trying to scare me," he shouted over the sound of his mower, "I just want you to know … it's working!" But Sam was the kind of person who, once he started something, was determined to see it through to the end no matter what.

As he parked the mower in his garage after finishing the yard, the Hastings truck passed his house again, driving the opposite direction.

I wonder if they have plans for this house.

Later that evening, he found his father in his workshop. "Hey, Dad, can a guy do anything if he thinks someone is trying to threaten him?"

"That's a tricky one because it's hard to prove. You can't exactly go around arresting someone because you *think* they might commit a crime."

"You can't?"

His father shook his head. "This is a great country we live in, but it's based on everyone following the rules. The laws are there to protect all of us."

"Even the criminals?"

"Sometimes."

"But like with this condemned thing. If a guy's guilty, he's guilty, right?"

"Yes, after he commits the crime; not before."

Later that evening, Sam worked at the computer. He wanted to read a little more about eminent domain. He found stories of towns that took people's property away so they could build a new discount store, a furniture superstore, and one town that wanted to build new homes where older ones already sat. A church had to give up its building in one city. Even though the owners were paid money for their property, it usually wasn't as much as they could have gotten for selling it to another person or business.

In every case, he read, *the owner had to sell and move out.* He clenched his fists, looked out the window, and gritted his teeth. "That's not gonna happen this time ... in this town. Not if I can help it!"

Chapter 10

Sam's Secret

No one could have suspected what was going on inside Sam's head. For all his friends knew, he had everything under control. That's the way Sam did things. But with the pressure building up, the threats from Hastings Development, and the fact that the days were quickly slipping away, Sam needed some help. He went to find his mother.

"Do you know where Dad is?"

She smiled. "I try to always know that, why?"

"I need to talk to him, that's all."

She placed the paper she'd been reading down on the counter. "Your father had to go to a seminar. He won't be home until late. Anything I can help you with?"

He shook his head and looked down. "Thanks, but it's the kind of thing a guy wants to talk over with his dad."

"Oh," she said with a bigger smile as he looked up. "One of those no girls allowed things?"

"Not really. I just needed to talk with him. Thanks anyway." He turned and went back to his room. Sam had a good relationship with his father. The two of them often talked about important things like growing up, responsibility, honesty, good choices, and the future. But time was running out on Mrs. Remmington. Sam had never gone up against a city or county before. In the past, they had always been partners in his projects. Now, he wanted to be careful, but he also needed some answers … quick! And that old queasy feeling was back in the pit of his stomach.

A little later, he told his mother he needed to go over to Mr. Kincaid's shop. Sam knew something his friends didn't. Mr. Kincaid wasn't just a junkyard owner who could fix old things. He seemed to know a lot about life and he was much older than Sam's father.

As he coasted his bike through the gate, Mr. Kincaid's big dog met him. Sam put the top of his hand toward the dog's mouth. Mr. Kincaid had told him that was a good way to greet a strange dog. Then the dog doesn't feel threatened. Blitz moved in closer to Sam's hand, sniffed it, and started licking with his big, pink tongue.

"Good boy," Sam said as he patted the dog's neck and the top of his head. "Where's Mr. Kincaid?"

"You called?" a voice said from the front door of the shop.

Sam climbed off of his bike, let it fall to the ground and walked toward the door. Blitz followed close behind, panting and slobbering in the warm morning air.

Mr. Kincaid wiped grease from his hands with a shop rag. "Your bike need another tune up?"

Sam looked back at it and then turned to Mr. Kincaid. "You did a good job on it, but a trash truck would be the best thing that ever happened to that old bike."

"Nonsense. Like I told you, they don't make 'em like that one anymore."

"They sure don't, and they haven't for a long, *long* time."

"If it's not the bike, then what did you need?"

Sam looked past him inside the shop. "Anybody else in there today?"

The old man shook his head. "Nope. Just me, all this junk, and Blitz."

"Then could we go inside and talk? I need to ask you something."

Mr. Kincaid motioned with one arm and said with a laugh, "Right this way to the executive office suite." They walked inside, across the room and sat on two stools next to a workbench.

Mr. Kincaid studied Sam for a moment. "You seem pretty serious today."

Sam nodded. "It is serious. I mean, this is one of the biggest projects I've ever tried."

"The Remmington place?"

Sam nodded again.

"But I hear you've done lots of big projects. What's so different about this one?"

"That's the problem," Sam said. "Everybody thinks it's easy, just because Sam Cooper's on the job. But if they only knew the truth."

Mr. Kincaid held up his hand. "Isn't this something you should be discussing with your dad?"

"I would, but there isn't much time, and he's stuck in a meeting all day."

"I see. Go on then."

"Well, I was wondering something."

"Uh-huh?"

"You haven't always been a junk dealer, right?"

The old man nodded.

"And you seem pretty smart."

Mr. Kincaid smiled.

"What did you used to do before ..." Sam looked out across the dingy shop area, "... before all of this?"

Mr. Kincaid smiled. "And this is what you wanted to talk with your father about?"

Sam felt his face getting hotter. He looked down, then said, "I've never had people try to stop me before."

"Who's trying to do that?"

"I can't say right now, but that's not the only thing."

"What is it then?"

Sam squirmed on his stool a little. "Well, people don't really know the real Sam."

"And who is the *real* Sam?" the old man asked in a soft, understanding voice.

"The real Sam is a kid who's never sure he can do the things he says he can. I mean, people expect it, but I don't feel like I'm the right guy for the job ... on any of the projects I've started."

Mr. Kincaid patted him on the shoulder. "Sam Cooper, the

longer you feel that way about yourself, the better man you're going to grow up to be."

Sam looked up into his kind eyes. "Huh?"

Mr. Kincaid nodded, slipped off his stool and walked to a corner of the work bench. Then he turned to Sam. "This world has plenty of people who are filled with pride about what they can do. They want everyone to know how important they are. He pointed over to Blitz. "You've heard people talk about someone who's all bark and no bite?"

Sam shook his head.

"It means they talk a good game but have nothing to back it up."

"Not sure I understand."

"Well, Blitz over there has a tremendous bark. You've heard it but if you do the wrong thing, he's got an even stronger bite. In other words, he can back up all that noise with action."

Sam walked over, leaned down and scratched the dog's ear. Blitz turned his head toward Sam and grunted. "You mean some people just talk, but can't do what they say?"

"Exactly. That's what's different about you."

Sam smiled. "What, I don't bark?"

"No, no you don't. But I hear you do get people organized and excited over the things you care about. You use your *bark* to get them involved and everyone knows there's a *bite* if they don't."

"I still have a hard time seeing myself that way."

"That's because you can't ever see yourself as others do. In your case, you might feel a little inferior in some way."

"Inferior?"

"The word has lots of meanings, but I'd say that you might feel less important, less valuable, or less worthy."

Sam stood up and he felt his body relax a little. "How'd you know that?"

"Simple. I used to teach psychology."

"You were a teacher?"

Mr. Kincaid smiled, "That's right."

"So what should I do with how I feel about myself?"

"The most important thing is to be aware of it. But I have to tell you, Sam, I've never known anyone like you at your age. And you should try not to feel inferior even though it's a good idea not to become too proud either. If pride takes over, then nothing you accomplish will be as valuable."

"It won't? Why not?"

"Because. If you change from doing things to help people into a person who does things so people will notice you and don't see the value of what you've done, then where's the good in that?"

Sam thought for a moment. "So, if I just keep thinking about Mrs. Remmington and how much she needs to stay in her own house and not about what a great guy I am for making that happen—"

Mr. Kincaid put up his hand. "But that's just it. You *aren't* the guy who's making it happen. Oh, you may get the fire started but it's all of the people around you who make things happen. You keep focused on that and you'll be a true hero, not the empty kind some people look up to."

THIS PROPERTY IS CONDEMNED

Sam stood a little straighter. "A hero? Never thought of myself as a he—"

"And don't start now. Understood?"

Sam nodded. "Understood. Thank you, Mr. Kincaid. Thanks a lot," he said over his shoulder as he raced out the door to his bike.

Chapter 11

The Best News

Sam's mother met him in the kitchen next morning. "Why are you up so early?"

"We've got tons to do and not near enough time to do it."

She brought him a hot, toasted English muffin to the table. "I've already heard several people talking about the new project. Your dad and I are so proud of you for what you're doing."

He smiled up at her, but his mind didn't even seem to be in the same room just now.

His mother looked at him more closely. "What's troubling you?"

He broke the first half of his muffin into several smaller pieces. "I don't know. All these people are depending on me. What if we can't get her house finished in time?"

She walked over and sat in a chair at the head of the table. "But once you get started, won't they have to give you more time?"

He shook his head as he put one of the muffin pieces in his mouth. "Mr. Hastings seems pretty determined to take it from her, I think." He gulped down his orange juice, finished breakfast and went back to his room to grab something before leaving to meet his friends. Back at the end of the hall, he heard the phone ring.

"Hello," his mother answered. Sam stepped back inside the door. "He's right here," he heard her say. As she handed him the phone, she whispered, "It's Mr. Grinwall."

He let his stomach do a couple of flip-flops before he said anything. "Hello, this is Sam."

"Sam. Good to talk with you."

"It is?"

Mr. Grinwall laughed. "After last night, it's good to talk with anybody."

"What do you mean?"

"Couldn't get to sleep. All I did was think about how bad I'd feel if anyone tried to take my house away."

"That's what I keep thinking," Sam told him.

"Well, if we can get your order delivered, say, early tomorrow afternoon, would that be okay?"

"Okay? *Okay*? That'd be great! Thank you, Mr. Grinwall."

"No. It's me who should be thanking you."

"What for?"

"For showing the people in this town what's important. Makes a guy feel pretty good to know he can help out like this. Yes, sir, mighty good. You tell Mrs. Remmington hello for me and everyone here at the building supply center."

"I sure will and thank you again." After turning off the phone, Sam felt like a tremendous weight had been lifted from his back. "You know, Mom, everyone's just gotta help now that Mr. Grinwall is giving us all that stuff."

"I hope so," she told him.

Sam smiled. "Gotta go."

He rushed out the back door, hopped on his bike and peddled toward downtown. This time, he beat the others. When Tyler and Tony rolled in, he could hardly wait to give them the good news. "You guys aren't gonna believe the phone call I got just before leaving the house."

"Couldn't have been *my* mother," Tony said. "I was still home."

"It was Mr. Grinwall. By tomorrow, his trucks are going to deliver everything we need for the boards and stuff that has to be replaced."

Tyler's eyebrows went up. "Really? Windows and doors, too?"

Sam nodded confidently. "And with the paint and electrical things, we'll have everything it takes to fix up that old place."

"Do you think enough people will show up to do the work?" Tyler asked, "'cause we're gonna need a lot of help."

"Hard to tell. I just hope all our posters and flyers did their jobs."

"Me, too," Tony said. "The three of us'd look pretty stupid out there all by ourselves."

Sam shook his head. "Not one of us knows how to build anything."

"And we'd never get done in time anyway," Tyler added.

Sam jumped back on his bike. "For now, I thought we could ride out to the house and tell Mrs. Remmington the good news."

The boys rode off on their bikes until they came to the top of Landon Hill Road, where Sam pulled to a stop.

Tyler ran right into the back of his bike. "Hey, what're we stopping for?"

Sam looked down at his front wheel. "With this bike, I always have to think about it first."

"Race you to the bottom," Tony challenged. He lunged forward and started down the treacherous hill.

"No, that's okay," Sam called out. "You guys can race if you want to, but I'm takin' my time."

Tyler pushed past him and yelled ahead to Tony, peddling as fast as he could, "I'm gonna beat you this time."

Sam eased his bike forward. It was hard not to think of his disastrous trip down this hill and how he could have wound up in the hospital, splattered on the side of a bus, or worse. He'd let his bike go just fast enough so he knew he could still bail out if anything went wrong. And the entire way down, he held onto the controls for his front and back brakes, just to be on the safe side.

At the bottom of the hill, Sam brought his bike to a stop in front of the sign.

Tyler pointed. "Hey, look."

"They changed it," Tony added.

"I know," Sam said. "Now they have the date when the house is supposed to be flattened."

"This is serious, isn't it?" Tony said.

THIS PROPERTY IS CONDEMNED

Sam kept his eyes focused on the sign as he nodded. "It just means we have to hurry. Good thing Mr. Grinwall made up his mind so fast. Come on, let's go tell her."

They rode down Mrs. Remmington's dirt lane to the heavy, iron gates. This time, they were closed again so Sam gave one of them a push. He opened it just far enough so their bikes would fit through.

About half way there, Tyler said, "Just think how great that old house is gonna look when we get finished with it."

Tony peddled around him and glanced back. "One more reason I hope a bunch of people show up."

"What if Mr. Grinwall hadn't said yes?" Tyler asked.

Tony laughed. "They'd all come rolling out here, ready to work, and nothin's here."

"Not funny," Sam reminded him.

Tony laughed. "I'm just sayin'."

The boys stopped at the front steps. As he climbed off of his bike, Sam was sure he heard a dog barking from inside the house.

Tony noticed it, too. "She must not know it's us."

They moved forward and crept up the steps like three scared rabbits. Sam saw the curtain open and close quickly. Right after that, the dog stopped barking. Before he could knock, the door opened.

"Am I ever glad to see you boys," the old woman said. Her breaths were short and her voice wasn't much more than a whisper. Sam looked down at her trembling hands.

"How come?" Tony asked.

"Because those mean men keep driving out here and bothering me."

Sam looked back toward the gate. "From Hastings?"

Her shaking head nodded, and she swallowed before taking a few more short breaths.

Sam turned back to her. "What do they do out here?"

She raised her voice a little, and it still quivered. "They walk around my house and yell things like, 'Only a few more days now' or 'We're offering you a fair price.' Sometimes they laugh at me, too."

Sam stepped closer to the door. "You don't have to worry anymore. We came out to tell you the greatest news."

"News?" Her face brightened. "What kind of news?"

Now a broad smile spread clear across Sam's face. "You'd better sit down first."

Mrs. Remmington stepped over to a large wicker chair on the porch. It had a faded floral pad and part of the back of the chair had broken out long ago.

Once she had settled, Sam said, "I had a phone call this morning."

She smiled and continued listening.

"Tomorrow afternoon, some trucks from the building supply center will be here with all the wood, doors, windows, and roofing material we need to fix up the outside of your house."

She sighed as she put a hand over her mouth. "Oh, my. How can I ever repay you?"

"No need for that. Everything's being given by stores and people from town."

Her lower lip quivered. "But … but why?"

Tyler chuckled. "If you knew Sam a little better you wouldn't have to ask that question."

"Oh, I wish Rudolph could be here to thank you."

Tony opened his mouth to say something, but Sam snapped his fingers just in time to stop him. Then he turned back to Mrs. Remmington. "We didn't want you to worry when you started seeing a bunch of big trucks and a lot of people coming out here tomorrow."

The old woman seemed a little confused as her eyes began noticing all of the repairs her house needed. "This is just too wonderful. I don't know what to say." The boys turned to leave when she said, "Wait. Would you like some cookies? I made them fresh this morning."

Tony rubbed his stomach and spun back around with a grin. "Never saw a cookie I didn't like."

She invited them inside and hurried to the kitchen. Then she returned with a heaping plate of oatmeal-raisin cookies and four glasses of lemonade on a tray. Sam shut the front door and joined the others.

Having the cookies gave the boys a chance to tell her about what they had been doing to help get people excited and involved in the project. After they'd finished eating, Sam thought he heard something. He set his glass on a nearby table, walked across the room to a large window and looked out just as a big, shiny black car drove into the front yard. Even though it was full of cookies, his stomach did a couple of its famous flips. The car continued around the circle drive without stopping, then drove back down the lane toward town.

Tyler and Tony came over and looked out the window, too. "Wonder who that was?" Tony asked.

Sam folded his arms. "Oh, I think we know."

Chapter 12

Here They Come

After the boys walked out onto the front porch, Sam said, "There's something not right about those guys."

"From Hastings?" Tyler asked.

"Right. They act like they already own this place," Tony said. "I mean, they come out here anytime they want."

Sam jammed his hands into his pockets. "I think it's more like an old western my dad was watching the other night."

"What about it?" Tyler asked.

"There was this cowboy, his horse had died and now the guy was lying out in the desert with no water."

Tyler gave him a funny look. "I still don't get it."

"Buzzards. They kept circling and circling way up in the sky, just waiting for him to croak so they could swoop down and …"

"You think Mr. Hastings is waiting for her to die?"

"Not exactly. It just reminded me of those ugly birds, the way these guys come out and drive or walk around the place like they know what's going to happen next."

"Kinda like they're measuring everything?" Tyler asked.

Sam nodded. "But it all changes tomorrow. I'll meet you guys here in the morning. Mr. Grinwall set the time. We can wait for his stuff to be delivered in the afternoon."

Tyler walked to the edge of the porch with a smile. "Yeah, and for all the people to come out too."

"I sure hope they do," Tony said.

Sam moved to the first step and looked out. "All I know is I wouldn't want to miss any of it."

The next morning Sam didn't even take time to eat breakfast. He stuffed a banana, an apple, and some bread into a bag along with a juice box. Then he left his mother a note on the kitchen counter.

I've gone to the Remmington Mansion. Should be gone all day. I took some food. See you tonight, Sam.

After that he hurried to his bike. The brakes had been slipping again so he made a quick stop at Mr. Kincaid's shop. Sam found him working outside.

"Do you always come to work this early?"

"Sure I do. Never know when someone might need something."

"Like me?"

Mr. Kincaid smiled and pushed his hat back. "What is it this time?"

"Same problem with my brakes."

"Push it over to the workbench. I'll see if we can tighten them up for you."

When they came to the bench, Mr. Kincaid took a wrench and screwdriver from the shelf and began working.

Sam continued to watch as he worked. "You can fix just about anything, can't you."

"Not like you."

Sam tilted his head slightly to one side. "What do you mean?"

"The whole town's buzzing about what you and your friends are doing to help Mrs. Remmington. It's a fine thing ... a *fine* thing."

Sam looked down and scuffed his shoe on the floor.

"Now don't be modest about it. Just remember what we talked about. This world needs more people who are willing to help others and expect nothing in return."

Sam looked up again. "I had to do something. I mean, what if it was my gramma or my mother? I couldn't just let them take her house away."

"I'm comin' out there myself to see if I can fix a few things inside."

"You are?"

"Wouldn't miss it for anything. I think you'll be surprised at how many people will be there."

"You think so?"

The old man nodded. "It's all people around this town want to talk about. A few of them have come to my shop, just to tell me about all the excitement."

"Well, I was only hoping enough of them would show up so we can get the work done in time."

Mr. Kincaid threw his head back and laughed. "They'll be there all right; lots of them. Don't you worry."

"Wait a minute," Sam said. "How we gonna feed all those people?"

Mr. Kincaid continued adjusting Sam's brakes. "Now there you go, worrying again. It's already taken care of."

"What? What's already taken care of?"

"You'll see." He stood up again with a big smile and tested the brakes. "There. Good as ... oh, that's right. You don't like to hear that."

"I'm workin' on it," Sam said. "Thanks for the help. I wish I could do something for you sometime."

Mr. Kincaid wiped his hands and shook his head. "No need. Now off with you." He waved his arms toward the open door. "Shoo!"

Sam peddled out of the shop and headed for the mansion. Since he'd started out so early, there wasn't any traffic on Landon Hill Road or any of the crossing streets either. It was too early for mail delivery and Mr. Elkins didn't try to back out of his driveway as Sam streaked by. When he rode up to the big house, it was clear to see he was the first one there. And he was also disappointed that Tony and Tyler weren't as excited as he was.

Mrs. Remmington shuffled out onto the porch to meet him. She looked down at an old, gold pocket watch in her hand and noticed the time. "So early?" she asked.

Sam still breathed heavily from racing down the hill. "I could hardly sleep last night."

"Me, too," she said with a giggle. "Of course, I don't sleep like I used to."

"Well, I wanted to be here when everything was delivered and all the people come."

"Are you sure they will?"

"We'll have to wait and see. Mr. Kincaid thinks so."

She smiled. "He's such a nice man."

"He told me that people have been coming to his shop just to talk about your house."

She looked at the peeling paint and other things that needed fixing. "This old place? Maybe they should tear it down, and start all over again."

Sam stiffened. "Don't even think like that." He threw his shoulders back. "This is *your* house, and we plan to make it look as good as new ... maybe even better."

The old woman shook her head. A small tear formed in her eye. "Land sakes!"

Around nine, Sam thought he heard the sounds of cars or trucks nearby. He stared out at what almost looked like the Fourth of July parade coming down the center of Harper's Inlet and now it was rolling right down the dirt lane leading to Mrs. Remmington's place. Soon there were vans, pickup trucks, and cars parked everywhere in the grass from the front yard all the way out to the street. Next, an army of people made their way toward the house.

Mrs. Remmington took a small handkerchief from her apron pocket, wiped her eyes, and said softly. "Oh dear."

Sam turned to her as more tears made their way down her soft, wrinkled cheeks.

First she blew her little nose. "I've never seen so many people."

Even Sam's voice choked back a little. "Looks like almost the whole town,"

A larger truck drove right up and stopped in front of the porch. Sam watched as Mr. Grinwall climbed out and stepped down to the ground. He slipped on a large pair of leather work gloves. Then he turned to Sam. "Would it be all right if I sort of take charge of this project?"

Sam could hardly speak. He nodded. "It sure would. I wondered how all the work was going to get done."

Mr. Grinwall turned back to the mass of people who came to work and began barking out his orders. As he did that, smaller groups of people scattered to different areas of the house. Soon tall metal ladders clunked up against all sides of that huge place. Some people began scraping chipped, faded old paint while others pulled off sections of rotted boards. It sounded like hundreds of giant woodpeckers tapping on the wood all at the same time. Others built scaffolding along one side of the house.

Another crew moved up to the roof where they prepared to remove old shingles and rotted wood. Those men set up safety equipment so no one would fall from such a towering roof. Sam watched in wonder while several other small groups cleaned around the yard. He heard chainsaws in the distance where men cleared branches and other brush.

Finally, Tony and Tyler rode up on their bikes. "Where did all these people come from?" Tony asked as he tried to see everything that was going on all at once.

Sam watched the workers too. "I know. I can't believe it myself. And there's just as many other people you can't see from here all around this house."

THIS PROPERTY IS CONDEMNED

The volunteers continued working right past noon. When Sam checked his watch, he looked out and said, "Oh no."

"What?" Tyler asked after throwing more damaged wood onto a trash pile.

"How we gonna feed all these people?"

No sooner had he said that when two white vans drove into the circle. Sam recognized the signs on the side of each one. They had come from one of the best restaurants in town. That's when he remembered what Mr. Kincaid had said.

Soon, long tables were set up with a huge feast spread out across them. People could make their own sub sandwiches from an assortment of meats, cheeses, lettuce, tomatoes, and any kind of toppings imaginable. Just the sight of all that delicious food made Sam's mouth water.

One section of a table held several kinds of chips and the dessert table looked better than the best birthday party he had ever seen. In no time, all the workers had eaten until they couldn't swallow another bite.

"We should do projects around town like this more often," one of the men said. Then he belched like a foghorn. Some of the others laughed.

Soon after lunch, several even larger trucks from the building supply center lumbered into the circle drive. Each had a forklift truck that was used to unload the wood, shingles, nails, shutters, and other materials Mr. Grinwall had donated.

Tony let out a long, loud whistle. "I'll bet you could build a whole new house with all this stuff." He took two steps backward and fell over a pile of old boards that had already been torn off the house.

"You'd better never go hiking in the mountains," Tyler teased.

A few of the nearby workers laughed when they saw what had happened. "Watch out for nails in those boards," one of them warned. "Wouldn't wanna puncture your … personality."

Tony looked up to him. "Huh?"

"Never mind."

By the end of the day, all the rotted wood had been replaced and the entire outside of the house was scraped in preparation for painting. Sam could hardly believe all of the progress they'd made. *But then, when have so many people ever worked together at the same time, in the same place, on the same project like this one?* He looked up and noticed that half of the roof had already been covered with new shingles.

As the sun started setting and the workers drove away that evening, Mrs. Remmington came outside. Her face gleamed and her eyes glistened.

"What do you think?" Tony asked her.

She giggled softly, reached up, and covered her ears. "I think a family of woodpeckers has been hammering on my roof all afternoon."

"I thought the same thing," Sam told her. "Tomorrow, they should start painting."

Tyler shook his head. "Woodpeckers?"

Same gave him one of *those* looks.

Mrs. Remmington kept gazing at all the work that had already been finished. "How long do you think that'll take?"

Sam ran his fingers over the new wood that had been nailed

up. "With all the people and equipment … only about three days, I think."

The old woman put a hand to her chest. "Three days? That's impossible. Won't it take more than one coat of paint? That's what my Rudolph used to say."

Sam pointed to a tarp in the corner of the porch. "Mr. Grinwall brought out a bunch of paint sprayers. He told me they'd put on the first coat by the end of the day. Then another coat on each of the next two days and all the trim on the third day too."

The old woman took her arms and nearly squeezed herself. "This is so exciting," she said as her voice cracked.

"Now if we can just stay on schedule," Sam told her.

"Schedule? What schedule."

Sam answered in a reassuring tone. "Never mind,"

As the boys rode away on their bikes, Tyler asked, "You mean she doesn't know there's a deadline?"

Sam shook his head. "I don't think so."

"I sure hope we make it," Tony said.

Sam thought for a moment, then glanced back at the house. "So do I."

Chapter 13

Trembling Under the Stairs

On the way home, Tyler asked, "You guys wanna come over to my house for a swim?"

Tony turned to him. "Now?"

"Sure. Why not now?"

Sam and Tony hurried to their houses to get swimming trunks and to let their parents know where they'd be.

"How did it go today?" Sam's mother asked as he burst through the door. He skidded to a stop. His eyes flashed as he told her, "You should have been there, Mom. People came from *everywhere.*"

"Will you finish it in time?"

"We have to. Is it all right if I go over to Tyler's house for a couple hours?"

"Are you going to eat supper there?"

"Probably. But we need to talk over a few things about the house."

"Sure. That's fine with me. Have fun."

"We will." He hurried to get his things, then ran back to his bike and headed to his friend's house. He had just gotten to the pool when Tony rode up on his bike and coasted through the open gate to the pool. "At least six people stopped me on the way here to ask about the house. That's why I'm late." He shut the gate, parked his bike next to one of the pool chairs, took three steps backward … and fell right into the water … with all his clothes on."

When he came back up for air, Tyler asked, "Were you planning to do your laundry at the same time?"

Sam laughed. "Hey, Tony, don't ever go into the roofing business."

Tony struggled to the side of the pool under the weight of his drenched clothes and finally climbed out. He placed the wet clothes on a chair where they could dry out, then turned and dove back into the pool.

Later Tyler's mother made sandwiches for the boys to eat outside in the warm evening air.

Tony groaned after his third helping. "I'm stuffed."

Tyler sat down next to Sam. "Do they start the painting tomorrow?"

"Right." He sat back and finished the last half of a juicy dill pickle.

"And that'll take them all day?"

Sam nodded, but his mouth was too full to talk.

Tony shifted in his chair. "Good thing they aren't using brushes. Those guys'd never get that job finished in time."

THIS PROPERTY IS CONDEMNED

Tyler thought for a moment. "Then after they get the painting all done and the yard is cleaned up, she gets to stay in the house?"

Sam finally swallowed the rest of the pickle parts in his mouth. "That's what it looks like."

"I can't wait to see the look on her face when everything's finished."

Back at home later that night, Sam did a little more research into eminent domain. Something was still bothering him. He began reading the site he'd saved about the organization that helps people when their property is condemned.

He stopped on one of the pages and read, "In spite of the United States Constitution and the constitutions of all the states, governments across the country continue to condemn property to be used by other private parties." He continued moving his lips as he read just above a whisper. "When activists get involved to stop their plans, developers find it easier to do their projects on other property. When a property owner is faced with condemnation, it is possible to defeat the plans of the developers, but it calls for immediate and swift action."

He looked up from the screen, then called Tyler.

"Hello."

"Hey, Tyler. I wonder what would have happened if my brakes hadn't broken?"

"What?"

"Yeah. I wouldn't have crashed into the fence."

"And you think that was a *good* thing?"

"Sure it was."

"How do you figure?"

"Well, I never would have seen that sign. We wouldn't have gone over to Mr. Kincaid's. He wouldn't have told us that Mrs. Remmington still lived in the house, and we wouldn't have gotten the whole town involved."

Tyler snickered. "Sometimes I think you think too much."

"Think so?"

Tyler laughed again. "Yeah. Hey, do you know if it's supposed to rain the next few days?"

Sam looked out his window into the dark. "No, why?"

"'Cause, you can't paint in the rain."

Sam quickly brought up a weather page and looked at the next ten days. "You're right ... nope. Looks clear."

"That's a break. Now if the painters can just get the job done on time with their big sprayers."

Sam let out a long sigh. "I'm sure glad we have those things."

The next morning, the boys were out at the mansion before anyone else ... except for Mrs. Remmington, of course. Right away, Sam noticed something that wasn't right when he looked toward one end of the porch. "Didn't Mr. Grinwall leave his paint sprayers out here yesterday before we all left?"

Tony pointed. "Sure. They're right over ... there ... hey, no they aren't. What happened to the sprayers?"

Tyler looked all around. "Maybe he had an emergency job come up."

Sam hurried toward the front door. "Let's see if she knows anything." He knocked, but there was no answer. When he knocked a little harder, the door pushed open by itself. He put his head inside and called out, "Hello. Anybody in there? Mrs.

Remmington?" In the distance, he thought he heard faint crying sounds.

Tony poked his head through the door. "What is it?"

Sam motioned. "Come on."

They slipped inside and began searching for the sound. Finally, Sam opened a small door to a closet under the stairs. There he saw a pile of coats on the floor and the sounds were definitely coming from someplace in there. He and Tony pulled coats away from the top of the pile until they came to Mrs. Remmington hiding underneath.

Sam hurried to pull the rest of the coats off of her. "What happened?"

"Oh … it was terrible," she whimpered. Her hands shook and her voice squeaked as she continued. "Just after midnight, someone came out here. They drove up the lane but never turned on their lights. I heard voices; deep, frightening voices." She took one long, deep breath and let it out in a wheeze. "I've never been so scared in all my life."

"Who was it?" Sam asked.

Now her breaths came in short, little bursts. "I don't know, but they walked right up onto the porch. That's when I hid and covered myself with all these coats. Never even had a chance to turn on the dog tape." She looked around the small, dark closet space. "I've been alone in here all night."

"Did anyone come inside?" Sam asked.

She slowly shook her head. "I'm not sure, I don't think so, but they made terrible noises outside. I thought …"

Tony leaned in closer. "Do you know where the paint sprayers are?"

"I don't even know *what* they are."

Sam pointed toward the front of the house. "They were those things on the porch under the tarps and now they're gone,"

Her voice became a little stronger. "I told you; those men were on my porch making all sorts of racket."

Sam pounded a fist into his other hand. "So that's it." After helping her out of the closet, he told his friends, "Stay with her. I'm going back to see Mr. Grinwall." He raced out the door and hurried to his bike.

"Take mine," Tyler said, but it was too late. Sam had already raced halfway down the driveway by then. He rode his old beat up bike faster than it had ever gone before. The wheels shook and everything rattled. When he was only a few blocks from the building supply center, the chain snapped.

"That does it!" he shouted as his helpless bike coasted to the curb. He pounded his fists on the handlebars. He looked around and noticed that people on the street where he'd stopped had put their garbage out for the weekly pickup. Sam pushed his bike over to the nearest trash cans in one yard and let it fall next to them. Then he took off running the rest of the way.

As he reached the building supply center, Mr. Grinwall was just about to leave with dozens of paint cans in the back of his truck.

"Wait!" Sam screamed. A minute later and he would have been too late. He waved his arms desperately in the air and cried out again, "Mr. Grinwall! Wait up!"

THIS PROPERTY IS CONDEMNED

When Mr. Grinwall slammed on the brakes of his truck, several paint cans slid forward and hit the back of his cab. He opened the door and climbed out. "What is it, Sam? I was just coming out to the mansion."

Sam could hardly speak for the first few seconds. He leaned down and held his hands on his knees. "Somebody … went out there last … night and stole all the … sprayers."

"Are you sure?"

Sam nodded. A feeling of sadness flooded through him like the time when his old cat died. Up until now, that was as bad as he had ever felt before, but this was even worse … much worse. He almost started to cry.

Mr. Grinwall must have noticed that too because he put a hand on Sam's shoulder and said, "Now, now. It's not the end of the world. I have a hundred of those things in my warehouse."

Sam's face brightened as he straightened up again, still struggling to catch his breath. "You do?"

"Sure. If they think stealing a few paint sprayers is going to stop this army, well …"

"I'm sure glad you're helping us," Sam said with a broad smile.

"This is one project that Hastings isn't going to block."

"Huh?"

"Never mind. Let's just get those sprayers. I'll report it to the police later."

Sam had to ride in the truck because now he was bike-less. On the way to the mansion he asked, "You really don't like the construction company people, do you?"

Mr. Grinwall shook his head. "What I don't like is greed. Greedy people can spoil things for the rest of us."

"Did they do something bad to you?"

Mr. Grinwall continued driving and looked straight out the windshield. "It was a long time ago. I was just a boy myself. That's when old man Hastings cheated my dad out of some property. It's the first and only time I ever saw my dad cry. The deal ruined us, and I think it's why he died so early."

Sam sat up straight. "Really?"

Mr. Grinwall nodded. Sam noticed a sad look on the man's face. "This isn't about revenge, mind you. I don't believe in revenge, but it is about not letting the same thing happen to that nice lady."

"So that's why you decided to help us?"

He nodded and looked over to Sam. "It sure is. And it's why I called everyone in town I could think of to help out."

"You did that?"

He smiled to Sam. "Of course. How else did you think so many people showed up … your charming personality?"

Sam smiled back. "We just have to get the job done in time."

"We will," Mr. Grinwall said as he turned down the lane, pushed harder on the gas, and rumbled toward the old mansion in a cloud of dust.

Chapter 14

Let The Painting Begin

As soon as Mr. Grinwall's truck slid to a stop in the gravel and dirt, dozens of men in painter's pants and hats rushed to help unload the new paint sprayers.

"Good thing you brought these," one of the men said. "We were about to leave for the day."

Another painter said. "Yeah, there's no way we could get the job done very fast with just brushes and rollers."

"And besides," a third painter added as he pointed to Tony and Tyler, "those boys wouldn't let us leave."

Sam smiled at his friends and nodded his approval.

In no time, several painting crews rushed up ladders and scaffolding and were hard at work changing that old house from an ugly mess into something beautiful.

"It's amazing what a little paint can do," Sam said. He had watched as the men constructed more scaffolding around the house so they could reach some of the higher levels. Two other crews used trucks from the electric company. Those painters were able to ride up in large buckets like the people who go high in the air to change lights or fix power lines.

Tony and Tyler helped carry fresh buckets of paint and materials to other people who were painting the porches, railings, and trim with brushes and rollers. Mrs. Remmington kept walking up to the window, looking out, and then wiping her eyes.

Another large crew had removed all of the shutters from the windows and doors on the entire house. Those were now lined up and even more people painted them with sprayers and brushes.

Later, Sam walked over to Mr. Grinwall. "What color will the house be when the painters are finished?"

"I see you're getting a little worried."

Sam nodded. "The first coat of paint looks … awful."

"Thank you very much," one of the painters said from high up on a section of scaffolding.

Sam strained his neck to look up where he was working. "Sorry."

Mr. Grinwall smiled. "Did you forget that the first coat is just a primer?"

"Primer?"

"It goes on to seal all of the exposed wood. Some of that we had to scrape and some of it is new wood that needed to replace sections that were rotten."

"Then what happens?"

"After the primer coat dries overnight, we come back and begin painting the real colors."

124

THIS PROPERTY IS CONDEMNED

Sam let out a long whistle. "At first I thought …"

"That it would be this ugly, dull, battleship gray?" another painter said from his ladder.

"Hey, watch it," another painter said with a laugh.

Sam looked up at him and smiled. "Whatever color you use; it'll look a whole lot better than it did."

"When we're all finished," Mr. Grinwall told him, "this old house will look as good as when it was first built; maybe even better."

"It will?" Tony asked as he and Tyler walked up.

Tyler flexed his fingers from carrying so many paint cans. "What colors will it be?"

"The main part of the house is antique gray. All of the trim will be white."

Tony turned toward the house. "Trim?"

"Around the windows, all the railing, places like that."

"What about the shutters?" Tyler asked.

"Black. And the doors will be a deep, dark red. With those colors and the new, black roof, people will want to come from miles around just to see how good it looks."

Tony looked back to Mr. Grinwall. "You really do know a lot about houses,"

Mr. Grinwall chuckled. "I should. That's why the building center does so well. I plan to put giant before and after pictures of this house up in my store so people will see how you can take an impossible-looking project and turn it into a showplace." He held his arms up toward the grand old house.

Another painter looked down from one of the scaffolds and winked at Sam. "That sounds better."

By the end of the afternoon, the entire house had been given a fresh coat of primer. All the shutters had their first coat of paint and the porch and trim had been painted once.

Sam tapped on a window at the side of the house. Mrs. Remmington came and pushed it open. "Yes?" she said.

"We're all going home now. I just wanted to remind you not to forget and walk out on the porch while the paint's still wet."

Tony laughed. "Yeah, that'd be dumb. Your feet would stick to the boards and you'd have to stand there and wait till we came out in the morning to get you unstuck."

Tony began pretending to show Mrs. Remmington how her feet would get stuck to the paint. He took three big steps backward like he had to work extra hard to pull his feet free with each step. But when he did that, he stumbled over a few open paint cans, tripped, and landed in the painters' drop cloths. They still had a lot of wet paint that had fallen all day long and Tony found himself covered in a mixture of battleship gray and dry paint chips when he struggled back to his feet.

Tyler laughed. "I'd stay away from the cemetery if I were you."

"Yeah," Sam said. "No telling what you might fall into."

Tyler and Sam helped Tony wipe some of the paint off places he couldn't reach on his back.

Sam finished and tossed his cloth on the pile. "Hey. How am I gonna get home?"

Tony looked around. "Where's your bike?"

"I left it by some garbage cans. With any luck, it's already taking a trash pile nap in the dump where it belongs."

"If you can get to my house," Tyler told him, "I've got an extra bike you could use."

Mr. Grinwall opened the door to his truck. "Anybody need a ride?"

Sam raised his hand. "I do."

"Well, I was just leaving. I'd be glad to drop you off."

"Could you take me by Tyler's house?"

"Sure."

Sam turned to his friends. "We'll race you,"

"Hey, no fair," Tony complained, but Tyler had already started sprinting toward his bike.

Tony hurried to grab his. "Wait for me."

Sam walked slowly to Mr. Grinwall's truck and climbed in. He couldn't hide the pleased look on his face. "The house looks better than I ever thought it could."

Mr. Grinwall started his truck and put it in gear. As they drove away from the mansion, he said, "With a work-crew like we have, there isn't anything we can't do."

Sam turned to look out the back window of the truck and shook his head. "I still can't believe so many people came to help."

"You know," Mr. Grinwall said, "neither can I."

"Do you think Mr. Hastings might still try something?"

"How could he? We're making sure the house is in better condition than even the law says it has to be."

"I know, but …"

Sam noticed Mr. Grinwall's hands grip the steering wheel. He held on so tight, his knuckles had turned white. "Look, if they try any funny business, we've got some lawyers on our work team. Now, you don't think any of those guys want to do this much work only to see a pile of nicely painted boards scattered all over the ground, do you?"

Sam tried to smile, but he couldn't. Something was still bothering him. A few minutes later the truck came to a stop in front of Tyler's house where Sam jumped out. "Thanks for the ride."

"You're welcome. See you in the morning."

"Oh, I'll be there all right." He slammed the door as his friends rode up.

All out of breath, Tony slid to a stop. "We almost beat you guys."

Sam slowly nodded. "Sure you did, Tony … sure you did."

Tyler went to the garage and brought out his extra bike. "I need to pump up the tires for you first."

Tony watched him push the bike out. "You mean they keep going flat?"

"Hey, at least it's a bike."

Sam looked at its dark blue paint. "Not a rust spot anywhere," he said. "Thanks for letting me use it."

After only a few minutes of pumping, Sam and Tony rode together down the street.

"Man," Tony said, "it sure feels good to be helping Mrs. Remmington like this. You got any idea what it would cost if we had to pay for everything?"

Sam sighed. "No idea. I just know we could never afford it."

When they rolled up to Tony's street, he turned toward his house and Sam kept going straight.

"See you in the morning, Tony."

Tony called over his shoulder as he continued peddling. "Yeah, see ya. I can't wait."

"Me, too."

Sam decided to take a shortcut. It took him through an area where several new apartments were being built. In one field filled with tall grass, he noticed rows and rows of gigantic cement pipes that would soon be lowered into trenches that had already been dug into the ground. He found a path through the grass just wide enough to ride his bike. At one point, he almost ran into two gigantic boulders hidden in the tall grass. He turned his front wheel at the last second and slipped safely between them.

The pipes were high enough that, if he ducked down just a little, he could ride his bike right through them.

This feels like my own Interstate tunnel, he thought. At the end of each section, he had to slow down, push his bike over the gap and then ride through the next long section. He did this through about a dozen pipes until he came to the end of the last one. He was just about to blast out of the final section of pipe and ride up onto a road when he saw something that gave him the sickest feeling he'd ever felt in his stomach.

Sam hit the brakes and skidded on a thin layer of sand in the bottom of the pipe. His bike came to a stop just inches before shooting out of the end and onto a wide open area where the grass and weeds weren't as high.

Next to one of the apartments being built, he saw a van from Hastings Construction. Two men stood beside it while they talked. Sam slipped off the bike and eased it down inside the pipe. He looked around and noticed another row of pipes running from where he stood all the way to just a few feet from the van.

After carefully looking around, he crouched down, like he was on a SWAT team and began moving closer to the men. When he finally reached the last section of concrete pipe, he could actually hear their voices.

Sam dropped to his hands and knees and crawled right up to the edge of the pipe. When he looked out, his heart nearly stopped for a moment. He felt a cold sweat all over because, not more than ten feet away, Sam recognized one of the men.

"Hastings!" he half-whispered.

Chapter 15

The Scariest Chase

Still crouching down inside the safety of that drainpipe, Sam's heart began pounding so hard he was sure it sounded like a big base drum in the marching band. His hands shook and he felt even sicker in his stomach. And that was before he heard what the men were saying.

"Things was going just fine until those drippy kids got everyone in town stirred up," the worker said. Sam peeked around the corner of the pipe and watched as the man took off his hardhat and wiped sweat from his forehead.

Mr. Hastings threatened, "You just leave those boys to me." He pounded his fist on the hood of the truck. From the loud sound, Sam was sure that his fist had just left a nice dent.

The other man spit on the ground. "But it ain't gonna look too good if they get it all fixed up and then we still go in there and knock it down."

Sam crawled across a small, open space and spotted a pile of rocks. Right then, he wanted to pick up a few and teach those men a lesson.

"What happens if they get it done?" the other man asked.

Mr. Hastings threw back his head and laughed one of the evillest laughs Sam had ever heard. "I think that's exactly what I'm gonna do."

The other man tilted his head to one side and raised his hands. "What, Mr. Hastings?"

He continued laughing. Then he looked out toward where Sam was hiding. "Let 'em finish the job. That'll teach them to keep their noses out of my business."

"Yeah, but you don't get that road built through there and you're gonna have a lot of explaining to do to the big boys up north."

Mr. Hastings took a quick look around and put a finger to his lips. "Shhh. Stop talking foolishness. If that happens, we're all in trouble."

"But you don't know these guys. I heard about one developer who didn't do what he promised and no one's heard from him since."

Sam gulped and he ducked down a little farther behind the rocks.

"They say the guy's buried under three feet of concrete in the basement of one of his own houses."

Mr. Hastings put up his hand. "Stop it," he demanded. "I already told you. With our friends on the city council, the county board, and ..." He looked around again to make sure no one else could hear him. "There's no way I'm losing this project."

THIS PROPERTY IS CONDEMNED

Sam peeked out and saw Mr. Hastings clenching his fists.

"Shoot," the other man said, "over half the people down at City Hall are in on it with you anyway, and all the county board mem ..."

"Will you shut your mouth! Nobody's supposed to know about that. If the news ever got out ..." He shook his head but didn't say anything more.

The man with Mr. Hastings put his foot up on the front bumper of the truck. "Well just wait till that dumb kid finds out all his work was a big waste of time and money."

Mr. Hastings chuckled. "Yeah, when we unload the bulldozer, won't he be surprised." He laughed again. "The ol' bat had better not be inside or we'll smash the house and bury her at the same time."

Just then, something horrible happened. It might have been because of all the dust swirling around the construction site since a gust of wind had just blown a big cloud of it right through the pipe next to where Sam was hiding. He almost sneezed at first and was able to stop that one from exploding ... somehow. But everyone knows how awful it feels when you absolutely have to sneeze in a place where you positively shouldn't. What Sam couldn't stop was a tickle that started way down deep. Anyone who has ever felt that tickle knows it's only a matter of time before an uncontrollable blast is sure to follow. Sam could try all he wanted to, but sooner or later, it was going to happen.

If I only had a water bottle. He began crawling farther back toward the entrance to the pipe and away from the men. Two times he almost coughed but when he swallowed that tickle went away. He moved quickly into the pipe, crawled to the middle and stopped. Then the third time he felt that tickle, it happened.

Sam let out such a sonic blast, it echoed all the way through the pipeline. He felt like trying to hold it back might have made it even louder than a normal sneeze and he thought it sounded like dozens of other guys were hiding in the pipes with him. When he turned back, he saw both men sticking their heads in at the end of the pipe where he crouched.

"Hey!" Mr. Hastings demanded. His voice thundered and echoed through the pipes. "What are you doing in there?"

Sam gulped and closed his eyes. Then he turned toward the far end of the pipeline. "Running!" he called back, looking more like a gorilla as he hunched down and scurried away.

Mr. Hastings ordered, "Get the truck!"

When he was only halfway back to his bike, Sam heard the sound of the van as its engine started up and the truck turned into the grassy field with a roar.

"This is so not good," Sam moaned as he ran even faster. When he reached the other end of the pipes, it sounded like the Hastings van might be only a few yards behind him. He leaped onto his bike and began riding away on the narrow trail that cut through tall grass in an otherwise empty field. He glanced back to see the van slide almost to a stop near the pipes. The door flung open and Mr. Hastings jumped in on the passenger side while it was still moving. Then it roared ahead again as the men began chasing Sam deeper and deeper into the field.

His heart beat like a frightened bird. And his dry throat made him cough so hard, he nearly fell right off of his bike a couple times. In his side, he began to feel a sometimes dull, sometimes sharp pain. *I don't know if I can make it.* But still he rode as hard as he could. *Glad I don't have my old, rusty bike.*

The van had to make a wider turn around the field of pipes. Mr. Hastings leaned out of his window and yelled, "Stop! You're on private property!"

Sam felt such terror, he thought he might pass out right in the middle of the trail, but he continued peddling as hard as his legs would let him. By now, the van roared not far behind him. The chase reminded him of a show he'd seen on TV where men on safari in Africa chased animals with their truck. Only in that program, it was to shoot pictures. Right now, he felt like the hunted and he *knew* those men weren't interested in taking a picture. His legs burned and ached under the strain. He felt a cramp starting in his right calf. Almost as soon as that one began throbbing, another started higher in his other leg.

Mr. Hastings leaned his head out the open van window. "You can't outrun us. We'll get you!" He pounded on the outside of his door again. "Don't let him get away!"

At first when Sam heard him pounding on the door, he thought they might be shooting at him, so he ducked down on his bike.

No one will ever find me. Then how will Mrs. Remmington get her house finished?

The driver began blowing the van's horn. That sound made an already terrifying situation even worse. Sam didn't take the time to look back. Then … just up ahead … he spotted something and it gave him an idea. He began riding in a zigzag pattern and the van followed his every move; first left, then right, and then left again. But riding off the trail only slowed his bike down in the grass, helping the van get closer. By now, Sam's throat was as dry and scratchy as the sandpaper some of the painters had used to scrape boards back at the old house.

Not much farther.

"We got you now," the driver called out of his window. Then he laid on the horn again as Mr. Hastings continued pounding on the outside of his door.

Sam could almost feel heat from the truck's engine now. "If they're trying to scare me … they're doing a pretty good job," he mumbled in a scratchy voice. His entire body felt drained of any strength or energy. It was all he could do to keep his wobbly legs peddling. Sam knew he was no match for the power and speed of the van. And by this time, they were almost on top of him.

At that very moment, he aimed his bike toward the narrow opening between those two large rocks hiding in the tallest grass he'd come through earlier. The space he remembered was only wide enough for a bike and a kid to pass through. Sam found an extra burst of energy as he streaked between the hidden boulders. He hoped the men were watching him and not where they were driving … he was right.

Once he'd shot between them and he was at a safe distance, Sam skidded to a stop and turned around just in time to watch the van race forward at full speed, and smack right into both boulders. After a loud crash, the van came to a sudden stop with the front end sticking up in the air. Sam continued watching as steam and smoke billowed into the air. Finally, the men struggled to get out.

"You idiot," Mr. Hastings screamed as he half fell and half dove out his window. "Why didn't you watch where we were going?"

"Me? You was the one yelling, 'Get him, get him!' What was I supposed to do?"

Suddenly, the van exploded in a ball of fire as the two men ran for their lives. Well, all they could really do was limp away on injured legs.

By now, Sam gasped for every breath. All he wanted to do was collapse into the grass and rest. But before he could even think about that, the driver got up and staggered toward him with his fist raised in the air. Sam noticed blood on the man's forehead and arm. He also ran with a limp.

Sam turned his bike and rode until he reached a flat section where he was able to ride even faster. Soon, when he looked back over his shoulder, he could see the man had stopped running, leaned down and begun rubbing his battered leg. Black smoke continued pouring into the sky. In the distance, Sam heard sirens. But he also heard something else—a hissing sound. That's when he looked down at his front tire. It was nearly flat.

He choked and sighed at the same time. "Good thing they don't know that."

When he reached his house, Sam decided to keep his little drainpipe adventure to himself. He strained to go inside, gulped about a gallon of water from the bathroom faucet and called Tyler.

"Yo!"

"Hey, Tyler."

"You sound all out of breath or something."

Sam rubbed the backs of his legs. "Yeah. Kinda."

"Where you been?"

"I … I took a little ride on your bike."

"Beauty, isn't it?"

"Sure is, but those flat tires can come at the worst time."

"Doesn't your dad have a pump?"

"I think so. I'll tape it on the frame tomorrow in case of emergencies."

"Emergencies? What can go wrong on a stupid bike?"

Sam rubbed one of his legs and groaned. "You'd be surprised. Anyway, I wanted to let you know I'll be a little late tomorrow."

"How come?"

"Have to make a stop first."

"You bringing donuts?"

"No, nothing like that. Just let Mr. Grinwall know, would ya?"

"Okay. See you tomorrow."

Sam didn't sleep very well that night. Those men had frightened him more than anything had in his life. He wasn't even that scared out on Lost Island. *They couldn't have been trying to kill me, could they?*

Then he remembered what the men had said, *"Yeah, you don't get the road through there, you're gonna have a lot of explaining to do to the big boys up north.*

"Stop talking foolishness.

THIS PROPERTY IS CONDEMNED

"But you don't know these guys. I heard one developer didn't do what he promised, and no one's heard from him since."

Those words sent a deep, cold shiver through him that made his whole body shake. It reminded him of the drug smugglers who chased him along with Tony and Tyler out on Lost Island. The dreams he had in the night made the scariest movie he'd ever seen look like a harmless cartoon.

In the morning, he awakened early and heard his father getting ready for work. Sam went to the open bathroom door. "Dad, I think I'm in the middle of something that could be dangerous."

His father turned off his electric razor. "That's one of the benefits of having parents to protect you," he said with a smile.

Sam swallowed hard. "I'm serious. Last night some guys chased me in a van. I almost didn't get away."

"They what ... who were they?"

"I'd rather not say just yet."

"You know them?"

He nodded. "And I think I know what they're up to. All I have to do is prove it."

Sam's father set his razor on the edge of the sink, turned to Sam and pointed. "Now you listen to me. Don't do anything foolish. If you need me for *anything* ... anything at all, you just holler."

"I will, and I've got lots of help. I promise I'll be careful, but I was wondering something."

His father continued listening as he picked up the razor again.

"What happens if people are trying to steal a house away from someone?"

139

"Same thing as if they steal anything. Why?"

"Just wondering, that's all." As he left the house a few minutes later, Sam hoped those men wouldn't catch him before he could find out what was happening for sure. After pumping up the bike tires until they felt hard as rocks, he rode over to the county clerk's office.

I have to find some proof. I've just got to.

Chapter 16

Finding The Evidence

When Sam walked into the clerk's office, he found Mr. Thomas standing behind the counter going over a stack of papers.

Sam cleared his throat. "Could I bother you for a couple minutes?"

Mr. Thomas looked up from his work. "Sure, what is it?"

"I was still wondering about condemned property."

Mr. Thomas put the papers he was holding down on the counter. "I thought we took care of that the other day."

"We did, but I have another question."

"Go ahead."

Sam looked around the office at the people who were already standing in line.

One of them smiled at him. "Mighty fine thing you're doin' over there at the Remmington place."

Sam smiled back. Then he turned to Mr. Thomas. In a whisper he asked, "Could we go to your office and talk?"

Mr. Thomas looked to the others. "Why so secretive?"

He pointed toward the office. "I'll tell you back there."

They went into the office and Mr. Thomas closed his door. "What are you so afraid of?"

"I can't tell you everything right now. I just want to know if people could hide what they plan to do with a condemned property."

Mr. Thomas shook his head and took off his glasses. "I don't understand."

Sam thought for a moment. "I think someone's trying to tear down the mansion anyway."

Mr. Thomas stood to his feet and walked toward the window. He turned and looked back to Sam. "You mean even after all your work?"

Sam nodded. "Only not just mine; everybody's."

"But how … who?"

"I heard someone talking and I think they have a plan to steal the house no matter what we do to it."

"Are you sure about this."

"Pretty sure."

"And you have proof?"

Sam looked down. "Not yet, not *real* proof. That's why I'm here."

"So what do you want me to do?"

Sam looked up again. "Could you go through your records? See if you can find out if a bunch of people are doing something together that's not right."

"People? Could you narrow it down for me a little?"

"All I can say is it involves some people from the city council and the county board."

Mr. Thomas shook his head and smiled slightly. "How does such a nice kid like you know about a nasty thing like that?"

A pained look came to Sam's face. "I just do."

"Well, I haven't heard anything and I'm the guy who should know. I mean, it could cost me my job." He hesitated as he put his hands out in front and tapped his fingers together. "Tell you what. You keep working out at the house and I'll see what I can dig up."

Sam's eyes widened. "Would you?"

"Sure. Now get out of here so I can get back to work."

Sam turned and reached for the door. "Thanks." But when he opened it, his legs buckled, nearly sending him to the floor. Standing in one of the lines at the counter, he saw the worker who had been with Mr. Hastings out at the construction site. The man had a big bump right in the middle of his forehead, one eye looked black and swollen, and his nose was red and purple. Sam quickly shut the door and spun around. "Is there another way out of here?"

"Sure, why?"

Sam wiggled his finger. "Come here a second."

When Mr. Thomas walked to the door, Sam opened it just a crack. "Do you know that man with the bump on his head?"

Mr. Thomas peeked out. "Sure don't, why?"

"After he's gone, see what he wanted. I'll bet it has something to do with Mrs. Remmington." He closed the door with a quiet click and Mr. Thomas showed him to a side exit, unlocked the door and opened it for Sam. "You take care of yourself."

Sam slipped out. "I will."

By the time he reached the mansion, painters were hard at work adding a second coat of paint all over the house.

"Hey," Tony called out, "I thought you were bringing donuts!"

"Donuts?" several people asked all at the same time.

Sam looked up at the workers. "Who said that?"

"We did!" they all called down to him from the scaffolding and from on top of the roof.

"No, I mean who said I was bringing any donuts?"

"Donuts?" others echoed from another side of the house.

Tony pointed to Tyler, who had a wimpy grin on his face. "Sorry. I was just hoping, that's all,"

"Did somebody say donuts?" another voice called from inside of the house.

"Yes!" several people yelled all at once.

Just then Mr. Kincaid walked around the corner carrying several large white boxes. "Come and get 'em!"

Sam had never seen grown men climb down scaffolding so fast. They reminded him of monkeys he'd seen at a zoo once when the feeders tossed in bunches of bananas. In seconds, the workers sank their teeth into dozens of soft, sweet, delicious donuts.

Tony could barely mumble as crumbs and sweet sugar shot out of his mouth. "How come you brought donuts?"

Mr. Kincaid opened another big box. "I just thought it was a little something I could do to help."

Sam walked over to him. "Thanks."

THIS PROPERTY IS CONDEMNED

"For the donuts?"

Sam shook his head. "No. Thanks for our little talk."

"You mean about confidence?"

Sam nodded.

"It's an important quality in your character. Too little of it, and you think you can't do anything. Too much of it, and a person finds a whole new set of problems."

Sam swallowed another mouthful. "Well, if you hadn't helped me, I don't know what I would have done."

"About the house? You're doing a fine job."

Sam shook his head again. "It isn't the house or all these people or the work they're doing."

"What then?"

"I can't talk about it just yet. All I wanted to do was say thanks."

Mr. Kincaid smiled. "Well, you're very welcome."

Soon after their donut break, the crews were hard at work again. Mr. Kincaid took his tools inside to see what needed fixing. By the end of the day, the house looked exactly as Mr. Grinwall had predicted. Sam knew that the job could now be finished in only one more day. He turned when he heard someone driving up the lane.

Tony called out the warning. "It's one of Hastings' trucks,"

The truck drove into the circle drive so slowly, Sam thought it looked like it could have been leading a funeral procession to the cemetery. It came to a stop in front of the house, but no one got out. Sam saw the man with the black eye and bruises sitting behind the wheel. After making notes on a clipboard, he glared out at Sam for the longest time. Then the truck drove away again.

145

Sam's heart started pounding just as hard as it had when he hid near the big pipe. He watched the van until it drove out of sight. Then he turned and looked at the mansion with its new roof and fresh paint. Now he was more determined than ever to keep anyone from destroying all that hard work. And he thought no one in Harper's Inlet would ever help on another project if that happened.

Mrs. Remmington shuffled out her side door to admire the new work of art. Again, tears filled her eyes and she fumbled for her handkerchief. "I wish Rudy could be here to see this," she sighed as she touched the handkerchief to her nose.

Sam looked down the lane one more time to be sure the Hastings van had gone. When he turned back to look at that beautiful house he gritted his teeth, *no one can stop us now ... not even Hastings*!

Chapter 17

A Desperate Threat

As Sam rode home with his friends that night, he didn't say much.

"What's wrong with you?" Tony asked, but Sam didn't answer. When he rolled into his driveway, he heard something coming down the street. His heart jumped the moment he noticed it was one of the Hastings vans. When it reached his house, the driver slowed almost to a stop. Then he sped away in a cloud of blue smoke, screeching the tires on the pavement.

"They know where I live," he whispered. He hurried to put his bike away and get inside the house. *I hope Mr. Thomas found something.*

In the kitchen, his mother told him, "You have a message."

"Who from?"

"Somebody at the County Clerk's office I think." She pointed. "It's over there on the counter."

Sam picked it up and hurried to his room. He read, "I'm still working on it, but might have something. I'll call you when I'm sure."

Sam looked out his window and whispered, "Wonder what that means?"

After dinner, he went straight to bed. All of his hard work along with worrying about Mrs. Remmington had worn him out. It didn't help much that he'd hardly slept the night before either.

He couldn't believe it when his alarm went off in the morning. If it hadn't, he probably would have slept till noon. Sam hurried back to the mansion on his bike.

About halfway there, Tyler and Tony rode up beside him. "Today's the day," Tyler said.

Sam smiled. "Sure is."

"Think we finally beat those other guys?" Tony asked.

"Looks like."

All day long, Sam kept one eye on his work and with the other he watched that long dirt driveway to see if anyone might come out to the house from Hastings'.

Later that day Tony asked, "We gonna make it?"

Sam looked at his watch. "According to the papers, we have three hours left." He looked back at all the painters. "I think they'll finish in time."

At around three in the afternoon, Mr. Grinwall walked over to where Sam cleaned up a pile of empty paint cans. Landscapers were nearly finished planting beautiful trees, shrubs, flowers, and grass. New stone walkways had been constructed along with railings on each side of the walk.

THIS PROPERTY IS CONDEMNED

Sam stepped back to admire everything. "It looks like an expensive hotel,"

Mr. Grinwall smiled. "Sure does. And it's all because of you."

Sam felt his face turning red. "It never would have happened without your help."

Mr. Grinwall tipped his cap back on his head. "You might be right about that, but it took a spark plug ... someone to get the whole thing going. And that spark plug was you."

Sam looked down.

"It's true. You're the town hero."

Sam turned his head away. "I'm no hero."

The painters had taken apart over half their scaffolding. Most of it was already loaded onto big trucks.

An hour later, the work was done. That's when Mrs. Remmington came outside. She clasped her hands together like someone praying and shook them up and down. "Oh, I can't believe this dream is coming true."

Sam put his hand on her shoulder and whispered softly, "I think it's the happiest day of my life."

She reached up and patted his hand. "Mine, too."

"Let's hear it for Sam Cooper!" one of the men called out. Everyone cheered, clapped and whistled. Tears streamed down the old woman's face and her eyes sparkled like diamonds. Sam had never felt this good inside before.

Then, above the roar of the people, he heard an even louder sound. From behind the crowd, a rumble of large trucks thundering down the lane drowned out the voices and cheers of everyone. When Sam spun around to see what it was, his eyes locked onto a huge bulldozer on a trailer behind the biggest truck in the line. All of the workers moved toward the trucks as they pulled into the circle and stopped.

Mr. Hastings climbed down from the first truck. He looked like a conquering general who had come to take prisoners.

Mr. Grinwall stepped forward and demanded, "What's the meaning of this?"

Mr. Hastings grinned with an evil look in his eyes while clamping his teeth on a toothpick. "Just come out here to take over what's mine."

"What's that supposed to mean?"

Mr. Hastings pulled a paper from his shirt pocket and handed it over.

Mr. Grinwall studied it first. "This says you own the property. How can that be?"

"I'm not here to explain it to you, Grinwall. By this time tomorrow, not a single board in that worthless, old house will still be standing."

Sam screamed, "You can't do that." He clenched his fists and lunged forward, but Mr. Grinwall reached out and grabbed him just in time. Sam continued kicking his feet in the air and swinging his arms.

"Calm down," Mr. Grinwall told him. "This isn't the way to solve anything."

"But he can't do that," Sam sobbed. "You can't let him."

Mrs. Remmington lowered her chin, turned, and slowly shuffled back to the house. Her shoulders drooped as she stumbled in the side door and slammed it shut … hard.

THIS PROPERTY IS CONDEMNED

Several of the workers let Mr. Hastings know how they felt. "Booo! Get outa here! Booo!"

Mr. Hastings held up his hands. "No use cryin' about it. The law's the law, and this place is mine as of," he looked at his watch, held up one finger and grinned, "right … now!"

The workers stood in stunned silence.

Mr. Hastings took a step forward, leaned down until he was only two inches away from Sam's face and ordered, "Now get off my property." Sam felt the man's hot breath on his cheeks and forehead.

One of his construction workers climbed up onto the bulldozer and started its powerful engine. Thick, black smoke belched from a tall metal pipe. After safety chains were removed from the trailer, and large, wooden blocks had been pulled away from the bulldozer's tracks, the operator began inching the giant piece of equipment off the back of the trailer.

Sam dropped to his knees and pleaded, "You aren't going to start smashing it right away?"

The driver raised a large blade on the front of his bulldozer as high as it would go and drove around to the front of the truck that had brought it. Its massive, metal tracks tore apart some of the new walk, crushing several flowers and shrubs that had just been planted and knocking down a section of the handrail.

Tyler's warning was no match for the roar of the bulldozer. "But there's an old lady inside,"

Mr. Hastings simply laughed. "Then somebody had better get her out." He turned to his workers and ordered, "A few of you men start moving her furniture out, too."

Six or seven of his men walked toward the house and knocked on the door. The frail, little woman came out and stared in disbelief at Mr. Hastings. His men pushed right past her and entered the front door. Sam thought she looked so small and helpless compared to the gigantic bulldozer and all those strong men with broad shoulders and bulging muscles.

Just when he thought everything had been lost, Sam heard another sound. He turned to see a line of police cars screaming down the lane. They roared into the circle drive, lights flashing, in a cloud of thick, brown dust. Sam's father climbed out of the first car. "Everyone just stay where you are," the sheriff commanded.

"Dad? What are *you* doing here?"

Mr. Thomas hurried out of one of the other cars. He held some papers in his hand. Sam noticed a smile on his face and the clerk flashed him a big wink. "I think we found what you were looking for."

Sam stood up again. "You did?"

Tony moved in next to Sam. "What'd they find?"

The sheriff stepped up. "Seems a few people in this town tried to pull a fast one on a helpless, little old lady."

"What are you talking about?" Mr. Hastings demanded. He held up his documents. "I've got papers, too."

The clerk stepped forward and glared at Mr. Hastings. "After our friend Sam stopped by, I did a little more digging … and guess what I found?"

Mr. Hastings fumed as he spit his toothpick out on the ground. "You tell me."

The clerk nodded. "Oh, you and the rest were pretty clever. Too clever if you ask me."

"Well, I didn't do anything wrong. I just followed the law."

"You're connected with some pretty bad people. Did you know that?"

Mr. Hastings looked around to the others. "It's my business."

"That's not entirely true," the sheriff said. "Mr. Thomas made a few phone calls."

"Yeah, who to?"

"I called the Attorney General down at the capitol. He was very interested in some of the names on the list of your associates."

Mr. Hastings lowered his papers. "How did you get that information?"

"I never would have looked until Sam came to my office." He turned to Sam and smiled. "Make a great detective some day."

Sam looked as his father smiled at that. Then the sheriff ordered, "Read Mr. Hastings his rights, and round up the rest of his men."

At that moment, it didn't seem so important that his father didn't buy him all the new things his friends had. Sam continued watching as Hastings' men were arrested. Right now, he couldn't be more proud of how it happened. And if there was a hero in Harper's Inlet, Sam thought it had to be Mr. Thomas.

Police officers swarmed around the men who had driven the trucks and others inside the mansion.

"I didn't do nothin'" one of them grunted as he struggled with two officers holding him by each arm.

"We'll sort it all out at the jail."

Mr. Hastings began pleading as he was about to be placed in the back seat of one of the patrol cars. "Hey, I can give you plenty of names … big names. There's no way I'm going down for this alone."

The sheriff laughed. "You're right about that. You'll have plenty of company in prison."

"What do you mean by that?"

"At this very minute, the State Police are rounding up about half the city council members, most of the county board boys, and a few out-of-towners."

"I'm ready to make a deal," Mr. Hastings begged.

Mr. Thomas shook his head. "No deals. What kind of deal were you going to offer Mrs. Remmington?"

Mr. Hastings hung his head as another officer pulled his arms behind his back and slapped the cuffs on. Then he was placed in the back seat of a police car.

Sam turned to Mr. Thomas. "How did you know?"

"They weren't as smart as they thought. Somebody hacked into my computer a long time ago. After I'd entered the correct information, they came in later and changed it. Everyone knows how behind we can get in the clerk's office. If you hadn't come in asking questions, I doubt anyone would have noticed until after it was too late. Might never have found it."

"Really?"

"Turns out they were pretty sloppy. I don't think they ever expected to get caught."

THIS PROPERTY IS CONDEMNED

Mrs. Remmington walked over to Sam. Her voice quivered. "How can I ever thank you?"

He looked into her teary eyes and smiled.

Then Tyler walked up next to him as everyone watched police cars drive off. "I guess not all pirates use ships out in the ocean."

Chapter 18

The Biggest Surprise of All

After the police had taken Mr. Hastings and his men away, Mr. Thomas walked over and sat on the porch steps. Sam and his friends gathered around him on the edge of large planters made of stones, filled with beautiful flowers.

Sam shook his head. "I still don't understand what happened."

Mr. Thomas took papers from a folder. "It's simple. Hastings cooked up this deal where he'd make money building the road. Then he went to some of the men in town. They all agreed to keep quiet if they could buy up the property on both sides of where the new road would be built."

"What good would that do?" Tony asked.

"As soon as a new road goes in, land next to it shoots up in value."

Tyler nodded. "So it was all about making money."

"That's right. I did some more searching and found that they'd done it before I was elected to the office. And they had to keep quiet, because if anyone discovered what one of them was up to, then that would lead to the rest of them."

Sam took some of the papers and looked at them. "How did they make it work?"

"That's the easy part. Hastings moved things around between his development and construction operations. Then he made sure there were more people on the council and the county board who owned property than the members who didn't."

Sam stood up and put his hands into his pockets. "Then every time a vote came up, the people with property always voted together?"

"That's exactly what they did. Like I said, if you hadn't come to the office with all your questions, just think what could have happened." He looked at his watch. "I gotta be getting on home. Good job, boys."

Sam and his friends went to the door and knocked. Mrs. Remmington came and opened it. "Are they gone yet?" she whispered.

"All of them," Sam told her.

"I wanted to thank everyone, but I was so frightened."

"So was I. We just came to tell you goodbye."

She straightened up a little. "Goodbye?"

"We have to get home for supper."

"But ... you mean now that it's finished, I won't get to see you boys anymore?"

THIS PROPERTY IS CONDEMNED

"Well … um … I hadn't really thought about that," Sam said. "I mean … all I could do was try to get the house fixed … you know?"

Her shoulders slowly sagged. "I understand. You boys run along then."

The boys jumped on their bikes and talked as they rode away.

Tyler looked back. "It is kinda sad, ya know?"

"What is?" Tony asked.

"We don't have any reason to be coming out here anymore now."

Sam looked back, too. "I know. Wish we did." His front tire looked a little low again so he stopped to pump it up.

Tony pushed his bike in closer. "You think they'll all go to prison?"

Sam attached the hose and started pumping. "Sounds like it."

Tyler shook his head. "I wouldn't want to be one of those guys."

"Me neither," Sam told him as he finished. They pushed their bikes to the top of Landon Hill Road. Soon after that, the boys split up and headed to their homes.

That night Sam couldn't sleep again. He kept seeing pictures in his mind of that beautiful mansion scattered into splinters all over the ground.

After a few days, life settled back to normal. The news reports died down and people seemed to forget about all the excitement. Then one afternoon, Sam had a phone call.

"Hello."

"Sam? Is that you?"

"Ye … yes."

A sweet, soft voice asked, "Do you know who this is?"

"Mrs. Remmington?"

He heard that familiar, little giggle. "Yes, it's me."

"How are you, and how's the house?"

"I'm fine and the house is splendid! Did you know they fixed up the inside, too?"

Sam smiled to himself. "I know."

"I was wondering something."

Sam nodded. "Sure, what?"

"Could you could come out here tomorrow ... say about four o'clock?"

"I think so. I'll have to ask my mom."

"Wonderful. You can bring your two friends too."

"All right. See you about four."

He hung up the phone and went to the kitchen. "You'll never believe who that was on the phone, Mom." Sam thought he noticed she was trying to keep him from seeing a grin on her face.

"Oh? Who?"

"Mrs. Remmington."

"How nice." His mother quickly turned away and Sam couldn't see her face. "What did she say?"

"She wants me and the guys to come out tomorrow."

"What for?"

"I don't know. She didn't say. Maybe something broke again."

Without turning around, she said, "Well, the whole town knows you're the right person to ask."

"They do?"

The next afternoon, all three boys met at Sam's house first. His parents were away on errands.

"What do you think she wants us for?" Tyler asked.

Tony joked. "Probably to tell us the painters missed a spot."

They rode carefully down the long hill toward the entrance into the mansion. With all the cleanup work that had been done by the landscapers, it was now possible to see clear through the trees all the way up to the house. Even the iron fence had been covered with fresh, shiny black paint.

Sam stopped his bike.

"Your tire going flat again?" Tony asked.

Sam shook his head and pointed. "You guys notice anything strange?"

Tony laughed. "Every time we're with you."

"No, I'm serious. Look real hard."

Tyler was the first to spot what Sam was talking about. "It looks like cars are parked all over in the woods."

"That's what I thought."

Tony rolled his bike ahead of the others. "Hey, yeah,"

They pushed off on their bikes again and slowly peddled down the lane. As they came closer, Sam noticed red, white and blue ribbons decorating the front porch railing. The bright colors stretched all the way around both corners of the mansion. "I don't get it," he said.

That's when hundreds of people streamed in from everywhere. They cheered and clapped as the boys came to a stop in front of the house. Many of them yelled, "Surprise!"

Sam looked all around. "What's going on?"

Mr. Grinwall stepped out in front of everyone with a big smile on his face. "Mrs. Remmington has a special announcement,"

"Isn't this exciting," one of the women said.

Then Sam noticed his parents trying to hide behind people in the crowd. He grinned at them and they smiled back. His mother's eyes glistened. "I thought you guys were running errands."

Several people laughed.

A few minutes later, Mr. Thomas stepped out from the big red front doors followed by Mrs. Remmington. For the first time, Sam noticed that the lion head door knocker had been polished to a shiny, gold-looking finish. And he saw something on the porch covered by a big, dark cloth.

Tony grabbed Sam by the shoulder and whispered, "You're gettin' a new bike … I just know it."

Sam pushed his hand away. "I am not, now cut it out."

Mr. Thomas held up his arms and signaled for quiet. "Mrs. Remmington wants to say a few words, but before she does, I have something to say. What you're about to hear is very good news … something the whole town can be proud of."

Tony whispered in Sam's ear, "Why would they all care so much about a dumb bike?" Sam stomped on Tony's toes. "Ow! What'd you do that for?"

Tony's mother scolded, "Shhh!"

THIS PROPERTY IS CONDEMNED

"If it hadn't been for three brave boys from Harper's Inlet, none of this would be possible." Mr. Thomas turned to the little lady standing just to one side. Then he motioned for her to come forward.

She cleared her throat and began, "A few weeks ago, I didn't know what I was going to do about Rudolph's grand old mansion."

"At least it has *red* doors," Tony snickered as he rubbed his nose. Then he started singing in a whisper to the tune of a very famous Christmas song, "Rudolph the red-door mansion."

Sam stomped on his other foot. "Eeeowww!"

Now several people scolded together. "Shhh!"

Mrs. Remmington swallowed a couple of times. "Excuse me, I'm a little nervous," she said with a giggle. "Like I said, I was wondering what to do. Now that you have so generously helped to make all of this possible, I wanted to do something for each and everyone in Harper's Inlet."

Tony rubbed his hands together and opened his mouth to say something. Sam raised his foot again so Tony decided to keep quiet.

"So I had a meeting with Mr. Grinwall and Mr. Thomas and now I've decided." She looked out across the crowd. "I know I'm an old woman and I don't expect to live too much longer. So, when I die, this great mansion is going to be donated to the good people of this town."

Now Sam scratched his head and looked around. He saw Mr. Kincaid, who smiled back at him and gave him a thumbs up. Sam turned back as Mr. Thomas walked over to what was covered by that cloth.

Mrs. Remmington continued. "I plan to donate the house and property to all of you … for a museum."

Now the people cheered even louder than before.

Mr. Thomas held up his hands for quiet. "We worked out a name for the museum. It took us a few days to have the sign made up. Mr. Grinwall was in charge of that job." Then he looked down to Sam. "Would you please come up here and give us a hand?"

"Bet there's a bike under that cloth," Tony whispered.

Sam put his hands in his pockets and shuffled slowly up the steps but kept his head down.

Mr. Thomas told him, "Pull off the cloth." When he did, Sam got a chance to read what everyone else also saw for the very first time. The sign read The Sam Cooper Historical Museum of Harper's Inlet. When the people saw those words they erupted in shouts, whistles, and clapping again.

Sam fought hard to keep the tears from coming. He made sure not to look at Mrs. Remmington or he would have lost it for sure.

After the noise died down, Mrs. Remmington whispered into Sam's ear, "Go in the house and see what else I have for you."

When he looked inside, he could hardly believe what waited for him there. Sam found a shiny, brand-new mountain bike with hand brakes and two gearshift levers. When he pushed it out onto the porch, he asked, "This is for … me?" It was impossible for him to keep the smile from spreading clear across his face.

Mrs. Remmington smiled back at him and nodded as she clasped her hands together. Sam hurried over and gave her a long hug.

Quickly the people went to their cars, vans, and trucks to bring picnic baskets, coolers, grills, and bags filled with food. Even their friend, Captain Jack, came with an ice chest full of fresh ocean fish.

"Hey," Tyler said, "it's not even the fourth of July."

Later, as the sun began going down and most of the people had gone, Sam said, "We'd better get going so we aren't riding in the dark."

Mrs. Remmington walked over to them. "Well, you boys can come out and visit me anytime you want to ... you hear?"

"We will. I promise," Sam said with a smile. He climbed onto his new bike as someone took the other one he had borrowed to their truck.

"Don't forget to feed your dog," Tony hollered back to her.

Mrs. Remmington smiled and called out, "I won't."

The boys rode out through the main gates and stopped. All three looked back at that beautiful mansion. Sam noticed that the awful sign they'd seen on their first day had been removed. Then they peddled off toward Landon Hill Road.

Sam pulled out ahead on his new bike and challenged, "I'll race you guys." He sped away as the others struggled to catch up. "Last one to the top is ... the last one to the top," he called over his shoulder.

He used every gear on his new bike and was able to ride it all the way up without stopping. After reaching the top far ahead of his friends, he sat back and waited for Tyler and Tony to get there. Now he knew that the real heroes were all of those people who had helped with the work plus Mr. Grinwall for donating the supplies and equipment and Mr. Thomas for searching his records.

No longer able to keep peddling, his friends pushed their bikes about half way up the rest of the steep hill.

Sam looked beyond them toward the mansion. *I'm sure glad my old bike crashed into that fence or none of this would have ever happened.* He smiled broadly.

- The End -

THIS PROPERTY IS CONDEMNED

More from the Sam Cooper Series:

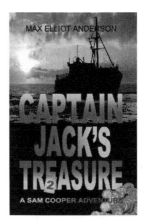

Max Elliott Anderson

40927644R00095

Made in the USA
San Bernardino, CA
31 October 2016